He felt her head lif

"Yeah."

But even as her arms slipped away, Tony turned, seeing again that refuge in her eyes he knew he was in no place to accept, no matter how desperately he wanted it. Saw, too, something else, something that blotted out reason but good, something that brought his hands up to her shoulders and his mouth down on hers, that sucked in her brief gasp of surprise and kept on going, as if by kissing her he could somehow glean a little taste of sanity in the midst of all this chaos.

Then her hands were on his back, kneading rock-hard muscles through his T-shirt as her mouth opened under his and the kiss became like a freaking runaway train, totally outta control, a rush to end all rushes, and he thought, briefly,

Definitely not little Lili anymore…

Dear Reader,

To say my family is small is an understatement—I'm an only child of an only child, with only one first cousin. My childhood holidays were very quiet…and, if I'm being honest, a little boring. But I married a man with three siblings, then went on to have five sons. Nothing quiet about holiday gatherings at our house, boy!

It's no wonder, then, that I love writing stories about large families. Especially the Vaccaros, who made their debut in my first GUYS AND DAUGHTERS book in November 2007. So when my editor asked if I'd be interested in writing another story about the Vaccaros for Special Edition's FAMOUS FAMILIES promotion, I was thrilled. Not only because it gave both me—and my readers—a chance to revisit this crazy, boisterous family, but because I got to "discover" a whole new branch of it!

So pull up a lawn chair, grab your beverage of choice from the cooler, and get ready to watch the fireworks as yet another Vaccaro guy runs smack into love when he least expects it. It may get a little crowded and noisy, but I can guarantee you it won't be dull!

Karen

FROM FRIENDS TO FOREVER

KAREN TEMPLETON

Silhouette®

SPECIAL EDITION®

Published by Silhouette Books

America's Publisher of Contemporary Romance

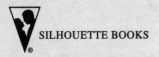

SILHOUETTE BOOKS

ISBN-13: 978-0-373-65470-3

Recycling programs
for this product may
not exist in your area.

FROM FRIENDS TO FOREVER

Printed in U.S.A.

KAREN TEMPLETON

A Waldenbooks bestselling author and RITA® Award nominee, Karen Templeton is the mother of five sons and living proof that romance and dirty diapers are not mutually exclusive terms. An Easterner transplanted to Albuquerque, New Mexico, she spends far too much time trying to coax her garden to yield roses and produce something resembling a lawn, all the while fantasizing about a weekend alone with her husband. Or at least an uninterrupted conversation.

She loves to hear from readers, who may reach her by writing c/o Silhouette Books, 233 Broadway, Suite 1001, New York, NY 10279, or online at www.karentempleton.com.

To Gail, for giving me this opportunity.
Did I say "Yes!" fast enough for ya?

And to my five boys,
for turning out to be such fine young men.
You guys haven't always made life easy,
but you've always made it fun.

Chapter One

Perched on a stool in a stifling New England kitchen that was not hers, chopping potatoes into a plastic bowl that was not hers, either, Lili Szabo thought, *Not exactly how I envisioned my life at this point,* orphaned and alone and vulnerable to things like spontaneous invitations to visit American relatives who, with few exceptions, she either didn't know or barely remembered—

"Are you done yet, sveetheart?" Aunt Magda yelled from across the room, and Lili glared at Self-Pity and said, *You. Out. NOW.* Finally it shuffled off, grumbling, and Lili smiled for her mother's older sister.

"Go. Enjoy your party, everything's under control."

"In zis house? Nefer!" Magda Vaccaro said, her heavy accent as proudly worn as her sculpted blond hair and theatrical makeup, even though she'd left both Hungary and the circus life behind more than forty years before. Her normal attire ran to tight pants and even tighter tops, but today she dazzled in a mirror-and-sequin-encrusted East Indian dress of tentlike proportions, worn with high-heeled mules and much tinkly jewelry. Next to her flamboyant aunt, Lili felt practically invisible in her white eyelet sundress. But then, most people disappeared next to Magda, who didn't need a spotlight, she made her own.

Then her Uncle Benny came in, Robert De Niro playing Santa Claus, to filch a sample of whatever Magda was setting out on a platter, stealing a kiss at the same time, and Self-Pity whispered, *I'm ba-ack,* and Lili sighed, suddenly weary of being the good one. The dependable one.

The cautious one.

"Any sign of Tony yet?" Uncle Benny asked, and Lili's head snapped up. Of course, in an Italian family, Tony was a common name. He wasn't necessarily talking about *that* Tony—

"Not yet," her aunt said with a sympathetic sigh. "But zen, he hesn't been on time to anysing since Marissa died. Such a shame."

Okay, so they were talking about *that* Tony. Except after all this time it was highly unlikely *that* Tony still existed, anyway, even if he hadn't been a recent widower—less than a year, wasn't it?—or the father of three little girls. What on earth could she possibly have in common with him now?

What did you have common with him then?

There was that, Lili thought, pretending not to watch as Benny swooped down on a laughing Magda to give her another kiss, sending a wink in Lili's direction as he strode from the room, a man happy in his world. And anyway—Lili slammed the next potato chunk into the bowl—if Tony was this late, maybe he wouldn't show at all.

Marginally cheered, she stood to upend the potatoes into a pot of boiling water, watching them succumb to their fate, ignoring Self-Pity's snickering in her ear.

* * *

"Do we *have* to go?"

His hands full of wriggling, giggling two-year-old—jeez, it was like dressing an eel—Tony Vaccaro could feel his oldest girl's frown from ten feet away.

"Yeah, baby, we gotta," he said, even though putting on the everything's-fine face wasn't exactly at the top of his list, either. But nobody turned down an invite to his Aunt Magda's annual birthday bash. And lived to tell about it. "Besides, it'll do us good to get out of this house. Interact with other human beings." Dress yanked over a little blond head, Tony shoved a hunk of his own damp, too long, not blond hair off his forehead. Josie seized the moment to bounce off the bed. "Besides—" he grabbed the squealing toddler, bouncing her right back "—you got something more pressing on your social schedule? JoJo! Sit still, for cryin' out loud, lemme get your shoes on—"

"Ohmigod. You can't let her wear *that!*"

Tony shut his eyes. Exhaled. Twisted to face the scowl barely masking the still raw pain in Claire's nearsighted eyes, the same pain that periodically throbbed in his own chest, that her mother had died and there hadn't been a damn thing he could do about it, that his little girl was still hurting and he couldn't do a damn thing about that, either.

That there'd been problems between him and Marissa, before she'd gotten sick, that had just laid there like a bleeping grenade between them, ignored until it was too late.

Then he noticed, framed by far too much light brown hair on either side of Claire's shoulders, the beginnings of a pair of somethings that had not been there yesterday, and his lungs seized.

Put those back, we can't afford them, hammered inside his head as a tiny person strangled his neck, peppering his cheek with noisy kisses. Got him every damn time, those kisses. Tony looked at his youngest daughter, wrinkling her nose at him.

"What's wrong with what she's wearing?" he said.

Grinning, Josephine patted the ivory lace bibbing the red satin dress she'd somehow not only found in her crammed closet, but had demanded to wear as only a two-year-old named after an empress could. "I'm pretty, huh, C'are?"

Claire shoved her blue-steel-rimmed glasses farther up on her nose. "Uh, Dad…that's a Christmas dress?"

"And your point would be?"

"It's *July?* She'll roast. Not to mention she's gonna get mustard and ketchup and crap all over it."

"Don't say c-r-a-p," Tony said, wearily, finally getting the baby's butt planted long enough to close the Velcro tabs on her glittery little sneakers—which even he knew didn't go with the dress—before setting the baby on the bare wood floor. Like a wind-up toy, she chugged over to the toy chest Tony had just filled to gleefully empty it again. "Especially in front of your baby sister," he said, dodging Super Grover. "And the dress is gonna be too small by next Christmas, anyway, so what's the big deal?"

Claire's hands landed on her hips, chewed fingernails dotted with her mother's purple nail polish. "Who the *heck* wears a Christmas dress to a backyard barbecue? Like, ohmigod?"

And who the *heck* was this kid? Swear to God, Tony never knew from one day to the next who was gonna come out of her bedroom door, like she was trying on different person-alities to see which fit the best. The grief counselor said the Jekyll and Hyde thing was a coping mechanism. Tony's money was on early-onset puberty.

"Don't say ohmigod, you know your mother hated it. But hey, you wanna try getting the baby into something else, go for it. Call Daph, wouldja? We're late."

Claire stomped back to the door, bellowed, "Daphne! We're leaving!" then stomped back to Josie's white dresser with a decided sway to her not-so-little butt that leached the blood from Tony's face. If she was anything like her cousins, one day the baby fat would reorganize itself into curves and Tony was gonna be a dead man. As was any boy dumb enough to get within fifty feet. "Mama said she bought that dress for me," she said quietly. "So maybe I'd like to save it for my little girl. Or something."

Ah, hell.

This had nothing to do with the baby wearing the dress. What this was, was Claire's wanting to stop her world from spinning out of control. Kid always had freaked out if God forbid they drove a different way to school, or changed a room color, or had spaghetti on Tuesday night instead of the usual Monday. Her mother dying?

Damn miracle she was functioning at all.

Wasn't like he couldn't relate, Tony thought as, baby shorts and T-shirt in hand, Claire hooked a zooming Josie around the waist and flung her back on the twin bed she didn't even sleep in yet. He'd kill for "normal" again. For what he'd had—they'd had—even a few years ago.

"Hey, JoJo, let's wear these instead—"

"No!" the baby said, arms crossed, matching her sister scowl-for-scowl as she pointed imperiously to the dresser. "Put back! Right now! I wanna wear *this!*" Then she scrambled off the bed—again—howling in protest as Claire grabbed for her. Again.

Tony's cell rang. With a grimace at the read-out, he answered it.

"Tony?" his mother-in-law said. "Is that the baby? Is everything all right?"

"Yeah, Susan, everything's fine. Minor fashion crisis, that's all. What's up?"

"Just making sure we're still taking the girls tomorrow. Although we certainly don't mind coming for them tonight—"

Josie's caterwauling ratcheted up another decibel or two. "Are you *sure* everything's okay?"

"Positive. And forget it, you don't need to be drivin' down from Boston that late. I wouldn't dream of puttin' you two out like that."

"You wouldn't be putting us out, honey, you know that." When Tony didn't answer, Marissa's mother switched tactics. Slightly. "Then…you don't mind if we keep them Sunday night, too?"

"Nah, of course not. The girls love it there, with the pool and everything. Not to mention you guys spoilin' them rotten," he added with a slight smile.

"Just doing our jobs," Susan said, her faux cheer wilted a bit at the edges. "You know, if we got them tonight, they could attend church with us in the morning, then go someplace nice for lunch—"

"Got it covered," he said softly.

"We're only trying to help, Tony," Susan said, just as softly, and Tony sighed, because they really were. And the kids were crazy about them. Not to mention their two-story colonial in Brookline with the cook and the housekeeper and that pool. And besides him they were the closest family the girls had, Tony's folks having both died within the past five years and his brothers and sister scattered all over the freaking country—

"Daph!" Claire shrieked as the seven-year-old came pounding into the room. "What on earth were you *doing?*"

"Gotta go," Tony mumbled, cutting off Susan's "Tony…?" His phone clapped shut, he slowly faced the child who looked most like him, with her dark jumble of curls and deep brown eyes.

Deep brown *don't look at the mess, look at the cute* eyes. "Daph, for God's sake—"

"I was watering the 'matoes an' Ed got in the way of the

hose, an' then he ran through the mud where I'd just watered, an' then he rolled in it…" Her eyes lowered to the mud-splattered devastation from the chin down, then lifted again. "An' then he shook."

Ed, their affable, terminally clueless boxer/shepherd mix—their weirdly clean boxer/shepherd mix, having efficiently transferred ninety percent of the mud to the child—grinned up at him, panting.

"So I see."

Her contrite smile punching dimples in round cheeks, Daphne held out grubby hands bearing a stack of smudged envelopes and catalogs. "Mail came."

"Thanks," Tony muttered as he took it, refusing to dwell on the muddy footprints Daph would have left in her trek to get the mail. Halfheartedly, he riffled through the usual assortment of bills, credit card offers and Don't Let This Be Your Last Catalog! warnings from Marissa's favorite mail-order companies, frowning when he came to the slightly damp, oversize envelope from their lawyer—

"You want me to change?"

"What?" Tony glanced at the walking, cute-as-all-hell mudslide in front of him. "Uh, yeah, sweetie. But hurry, we're sposedta be there by five."

"Won't take but a sec," Daphne said, bounding down the hall to her room, as Tony clamped the rest of the mail under his arm to tear open the envelope from the lawyer. Inside was a short note on Phil's letterhead, wrapped around another sealed envelope…addressed to him in Rissa's handwriting.

"Tony," he silently read over the loud rushing in his ears, "I have no idea what this is about, but Rissa asked me to send it to you when she'd been gone at least six months. I know it's been more like nine, but frankly, I forgot about it until now. If you need me for anything, let me know. Phil."

What I need is a new lawyer, Tony thought, turning to Claire, who'd apparently—since the baby was still a vision in satin and lace—given up the good fight. "Let me dump this stuff on my desk, then we can get outta here, okay?"

Except he'd barely reached the small bedroom office at the end of the hall before he ripped open the second envelope and skimmed the letter.

Twice.

"...I'm so sorry, and I know this is taking the chicken's way out, but I just couldn't figure out a good time to tell you..."

"Dad? You okay?"

The letter clutched in his hand, Tony wheeled on a frowning Claire, standing in the hall with the baby perched on her hip.

"Sure. Fine." Swallowing back the howl lodged at the base of his throat, he crossed to the battle-scarred Melamine desk to stash the letter in the top drawer, then fumbled for the Super Dad switch in his brain before turning back, game face firmly in place. "You guys all ready to go?"

"You sound funny—"

"Somethin' caught in my throat," Tony pushed out, thinking...nine months ago? He thought he'd been through hell.

Turns out he'd barely gotten through the front door.

Fine. If Dad wanted to pretend everything was cool, Claire could, too. Except she knew when he was faking being okay and when he was really okay. Not that he'd been *really* okay since Mom died, but she knew he was trying his best. For their sakes. Because kids weren't supposed to be sad, or something lame like that. Whatever.

Then he said they were gonna *walk* the six blocks to Aunt Magda's and Uncle Benny's, and she heard herself say, "Are you *kidding* me? You want us to die of sunstroke or what?"

"You've all got hats," Dad said, sounding mostly normal again as he struggled to get the Empress—that's what they sometimes called JoJo, on account of her being named after some dude's wife two centuries ago—into her stroller. "I think you'll survive six blocks. Think of it as being ecologically responsible."

"Or cheap," Claire grumbled with a longing look over her shoulder at their old Volvo wagon, sitting in the driveway. One fist wrapped around the stroller handle, Dad tugged a receipt out of his jeans pocket and handed it over.

"What's this?"

"That's how much it cost me to gas up the car yesterday."

"Holy crap."

"Don't—" He sighed. "Yeah."

Then it occurred to Claire that maybe she should cut Dad some slack, since this obviously wasn't one of his better days. "C'n I push?" she asked, reaching for the stroller. Yeah, Josie could be a pain in the butt, but she could be really cute and lovey and stuff, too. And Claire tried to help out with her little sisters as much as possible, so Dad wouldn't feel like he had to do everything. Especially since she'd overheard Nana and Gramps talking about how it would be so much easier on Dad if Claire and her sisters came to live with them. She loved her grandparents and all, but…no.

"Go for it," Dad said, moving over so Claire could take the stroller.

"The walk will do us good," she said, feeling all tingly inside when Dad's hand landed on the back of her head. She looked up at him, smiling, letting out a little breath of relief when he smiled back. Even if it was the kind of smile that made Claire's insides hurt. Basically Dad was pretty cool, if a little crazy sometimes, although they didn't see the crazy so much now. As awful as Claire'd felt when Mom died? She knew it'd hurt Dad a hundred million times more.

Which was why she couldn't tell Dad about how she'd found Mom crying one day, before they knew she was sick. Mom made her swear to never say anything to Dad, or anybody else, that it was a secret.

Claire didn't much like keeping secrets—they always made her feel like when you want to throw up but you can't because you're in school or church or someplace. But Mom said it would only upset Dad if he found out, so Claire said okay. And Claire never, ever broke her promises.

Even ones she was sorry she'd made.

Daphne's hot—but clean—hand in Tony's, they walked the six blocks underneath a bleached sky, the hot, sticky silence broken only by the stroller's bumping over the cracks in the old sidewalk and Josie's babbling. Not a leaf stirred in the sycamore trees fronting the sturdy New England Victorians, erected a century ago when families were huge and building materials cheap. The early summer humidity clung to everything like plastic wrap; Marissa hated this weather, the way her hair would always corkscrew into a tangled, frizzy mess—

The memory slashed through Tony like a rusty knife, re-opening still-infected wounds, now rancid with disbelief and shock. His pace slowed when his aunt and uncle's house loomed into view a half block ahead. How could he do this, go to some party and pretend like everything was fine when his guts were bleeding all over the damn place? But what choice did he have? Especially since turning back would mean facing a barrage of questions from Little Miss Never-Miss-a-Thing pushing the stroller.

So he'd do the playacting thing for a couple hours. At least the kids would get fed. One less thing to worry about, he thought as they approached the old brick foursquare where Benny and Magda had raised six kids.

Uncle Benny opened the door, immediately pulling Tony into a brief, but deadly, bear hug as a stiff-legged golden retriever and a cotton ball toy poodle eagerly rushed the kids, woofing and yipping and wriggling and licking. From every corner of the house, laughter taunted him.

"You made it," Benny said, clapping Tony on the back before Tony squatted to spring Josie from her stroller while the other girls hovered nearby. "We were beginning to think you wouldn't show. Aww…gimme the little cutie," he said, holding out his arms to Josie, who clung more tightly to Tony, shaking her head. His uncle laughed, not in the least offended.

Instead he grinned at the girls. "God, you two are getting so big! Unbelievable, huh? Hey—most of your cousins are upstairs. Even Stacey," he said to Claire. "You should go on up."

Daphne the Invincible was gone in a flash, but Claire hung back, forehead creased, eyes worried, obviously picking up on stuff Tony did not want her picking up on. Now or ever. Looping an arm around her shoulders, Tony wondered how soon they could leave. "Stace is here? So Rudy and them came down?"

"Just for the day. They had to find somebody to watch the inn." Benny smiled for Claire. "Stace was askin' about you, wonderin' if you'd be here."

Claire's eyes shifted to Tony's, torn. "Go," Tony said with a little smile. And a not-so-little push. Because if he had a hope in hell of getting through the next couple of hours, he had to stay out of range of that all-too-knowing look.

"Hey, Tone," Benny asked as Claire finally trudged off. "You okay?"

"Yeah, sure, I'm fine—"

"Tony?"

His head jerked up, toward a voice he hadn't heard in a thousand years and a pair of blue eyes as laser-sharp as he remembered, and before he could catch his breath Josie wriggled to get down, then ran over to this woman she'd never seen in her life. Her arms wrapped around Lili Szabo's knees, she looked up at her adoringly, and Tony felt like somebody had just shoved him off a damn cliff.

Chapter Two

"Oh my goodness," Lili said, her smile threatening to fry what was left of Tony's brain as she lifted Josie into her arms. "Is she yours? She's adorable—"

"What on earth are you doin' here?" Her smile faltered, and Tony felt like a jerk. A blindsided jerk, but a jerk all the same. "I'm sorry, that came out bad, but, damn—"

"No, it's okay," she said, hiking Ms. Chunkers higher on her hip. A hip much more, um, *there* than he remembered.

"How long has it been?" he asked, realizing Benny had disappeared. "Twelve years?"

The smile flickered to life again, giving him a flash of the slightly crooked eyeteeth she'd been so self-conscious about. God knows why. "Fourteen, actually."

"Fourteen. Right. God." He paused. "So what brings you back?"

"My mother died," she said softly, swinging Josie from side to side, making her laugh. "A month ago—"

"Jeez…I'm sorry—"

"It's okay, it wasn't unexpected," she said in her pretty accent. "A blessing, actually, when she finally let go. In any case, afterward…" She touched her forehead to the baby's. "I thought the change would do me good."

She was still skinny, mostly, except for a couple of crucial places that weren't, judging from the way that dress was fitting. And it wasn't like she'd turned into a bombshell or anything, because she hadn't, she was still just little cousin Lili with the too-wide mouth and long, ordinary brown hair that curved slightly on the ends. Although the glasses were rimless now, and her mouth seemed fuller or something—

"Tony? Are you feeling all right?"

—but she'd been the only person, Tony now realized in such a rush he got dizzy, who'd ever really *gotten* him. At least, the eighteen-year-old "him" who'd been so cocksure about what he wanted.

And that hadn't included his fifteen-year-old, slightly geeky Hungarian cousin visiting for the summer after her father died and the rest of her family toured Europe with their high-wire act. The only person, friend or relative, willing to keep him company when a stupid-ass skateboard accident shattered his leg, his summer and whatever hope he'd had of going all the way with Marissa Pellegrino.

Who he *had* wanted, with a single-mindedness bordering on obsessive.

"It's been a rough few months," he said, the words out of his mouth before he had any clue they were there, and Lili gave him that same disingenuous smile that had kept a cooped-up boy from totally losing it that summer, a moment before she gave him a one-armed hug…and she was soft and warm and strong and giving, no longer smelling of grape soda and potato chips but of something sweet and musky and honest, a scent way past dangerous to a battered, stunned man whose life kept falling in the crapper.

Then she leaned back slightly, her hand still on his arm, drawing him into the calm behind that smile, and he knew the exact instant when she saw what nobody else did, when those deep blue eyes said, *Come in out of the storm, where it's safe.*

As if.

I know that look, Lili thought, her Empathy Alert System spiking to at least orange level as she gazed into those dark, haunted eyes and saw a man struggling not to fall apart in public—

"She's probably getting pretty heavy," he said, taking the baby from her.

—rather than, say, the slightly dulled, stoic grief of someone who'd lost the love of his life several months before.

A thought which did nothing to mitigate the flush still stinging her chest and cheeks from before she'd stumbled into all that sadness and shock, when she'd spotted Tony across the room and her brain simply stood aside and gave her hormones the floor, those rowdy hooligans yelling *Taller! Broader! And did you notice the mouth, perchance?* in her ear.

Can we say, inappropriate?

Not that she and Tony were real cousins, since her parents and Tony's weren't related to each other, except by Magda and Benny's marriage. Not a single gene shared, anywhere. Still. What hadn't been right then still wasn't right now. Her hugging him, that is. Because they never had before. Although it was no big deal, everybody hugged and kissed in this family, that was just the way with these Mediterranean types, even those three generations removed from the home country.

And the tingling would subside. Eventually.

As would the instant, mortifying reversion to lovesick teenager indulging a forbidden fantasy.

"How old is she?" Lili said, smiling, unable to keep from touching the silky blond hair. To keep the slight sting of longing at bay.

"I'm this many," the little girl said, holding up two fingers.

"Oooh, big girl. And what's your name?"

"Josie. You're pretty."

Lili flushed even more. "Thank you, sweet lamb. So are you."

"I know," she said, and Lili laughed, before some female cousin Lili didn't really know carted off the child—Tony's gaze followed, protective and sad—and then it was just the two of them, awkward and bufferless.

Then Tony smiled for her, a very different smile from those he'd first spared for her that summer, when his entertainment options had been reduced to hanging out with a younger cousin who wasn't even cool by Hungarian standards. "Wow. It's really you."

"It really is."

But he'd never been snide or condescending. And by the end of the summer, the smiles had come more readily, as well as the conversations and laughter, easing Lili's chronic awkwardness. No surprise, then, that she'd developed a huge crush on him. Except he'd had a girlfriend and she was going back to Hungary, anyway, and…well.

The crush, thank God, had eventually faded. The memory of all that kindness and patience and honesty, however, hadn't. That he should be going through such hell now broke her heart.

"You have other children?" she asked.

"Yeah," he breathed out. "Two more girls. They're around somewhere, I'm sure you'll meet them."

"I'm sure I will." Then she said, "I'm so sorry about Marissa," and Tony actually jerked, the pain blossoming anew in his eyes as his mouth flattened into a grim line, and she thought, *Put a foot in it, why not?*

But before she could think of some way out of the tangle she was rapidly making of the conversation, she was nearly thrown off balance when her—their—aunt wrapped one arm around Lili's waist, releasing enough perfume to fell oxen at twenty kilometers.

"Tony, sveetheart! You made it! Now my birthday is complete."

Lili watched, amazed, as Tony seemed to shrug off his pain like an ill-fitting coat, then leaned over to kiss their aunt on the cheek. A move which brought his pheromones close enough to wink at Lili's hormones, those sad, neglected things. "Like I'd miss it, Aunt Mag."

Their aunt laughed, then squeezed Lili's waist. Harder. "And hesn't our Lili turned into a lovely young voman?"

Oh, dear, Lili thought, until Tony leveled an unexpected, and unnervingly steady, gaze on her and said, "Yes. She certainly has," and she could barely hear for all the stampeding hormones.

Before they trampled her to death, she spun around and ran.

"No, you come vis me," Magda said when Tony started after Lili, instead steering him toward the back of the house.

"But—"

"She'll come out ven she's ready. Like a kitty from under ze bed."

His aunt gently pushed him out onto the deck, the clinkety-clanking of a dozen bangles mingling with the roar of count-less gabbing Vaccaros, where the summertime smells of freshly cut grass and seared meat and beer taunted him with their overtones of joviality and predictability and normalcy. Trying to ignore the hot, sudden sting of sexual awareness, he scanned the crowd of husbands and wives and kids—laughing and arguing and fussing at each other—jealous as all hell and not even trying to deny it.

"Why's Lili here?" he said, more sharply than he probably should've.

"Is a long story," Magda said with a tinkly wave. "You can esk her yourself, later. For me?" she squealed, when another of her kids arrived bearing grandchildren and presents.

She'd barely floated off when a hearty clap on Tony's shoulder blasted him out of his thoughts—Rudy Vaccaro, big as a damn mountain and the cousin closest in age to Tony. They'd hung out a lot together, both as kids and after, and Tony had really missed the bastard since he'd moved. Rudy pressed an ice-cold, and very welcome, Bud into Tony's hand. "Good to see you, man."

"Yeah. You, too. Only don't even think about asking me how I'm doing." Rudy would understand the warning. And not question it. Still, below a buzz cut that should've made him look a lot scarier than it did, sympathy swam in sharp blue eyes.

"Wouldn't dream of it," he said as Violet, his still-new, cute-as-a-bug wife came up beside him.

"C'mere, you…" Violet yanked Tony down for a hug, her mess of orange curls ticking his chin before she let go, giving him a shrewd look. "How're the girls?"

"Doin' okay," Tony said, scanning the crowd for Lili. Not having a clue why. "Considering."

"Saw the baby earlier," Violet said. "Celeste was showin' her off like she was her own. God, she looks exactly like you. Except for the blond hair, obviously," she added, having no idea her words were like an ice pick to the heart.

Rudy lifted his own beer to Tony. "You and the girls should come up for a cuppla days—"

"Absolutely!" Violet said when Tony demurred. "We're booked most weekends, but we sometimes have openings during the week. And you're off from school all summer, right? It would do the girls good. And the boys would love it!"

"Yeah, Stace would be in heaven, havin' all those kids to boss around. God, I thought thirteen was a pain-in-the-ass, that's nothin' compared with fourteen. If we ever have another kid?" Rudy pulled his wife close. "And it's a girl? I'm seriously considering shipping her off to boardin' school between the ages of twelve and eighteen."

"Oh, right, you'd curl up in a ball and die if Stace wasn't around…"

Violet's jabbering faded to white noise when Tony spotted Lili creeping out onto the deck, arms crossed and eyes darting around the yard, and the stinging started up again, bad, *real* bad, bad enough to sound some heavy-duty alarms—

"Excuse me, I need to, uh…"

Run like hell. Throw up. Have my head examined.

Rudy and Violet's heads turned as one, then back. Matching grins. Hell.

"Hey," Rudy said, "you should bring Lili with you. She said she's never been to New Hampshire." Tony gawked at the man like he'd lost it. "What? It's not like I'm suggesting something untoward or anything. And anyway, in a cuppla weeks," he added with a discreet nod toward his mother, "she might need some serious rescuing."

"Yeah, yeah, I'll think about it, thanks," Tony muttered, giving Rudy a final arm slap and heading toward Lili—who'd clearly seen him—before she could bolt.

Except…this was nuts, this was just *Lili,* for God's sake, all that stuff about her getting him—or whatever—was just his sleep-and-sex-deprived, shocked brain shorting out. Playing tricks. Really dirty tricks. So he'd talk to her, right? Clear this whole crazy thing up.

Except as he closed the gap between them, he saw her take a deep breath, then smile, a smile that said, *I don't understand, either,* and a little voice inside him said, *Maybe not so crazy.* Which could only mean he was one step removed from certifiable.

And yet, he kept walking.

Lili stood, frozen, watching Tony charge toward her, telling herself she wasn't afraid of him, exactly, it was her own messed-up feelings—feelings perhaps dismissed a bit prematurely—giving her pause.

Especially when he marched up to her, all dark in the face, growling, "Why'd you run off?"

"Don't be ridiculous, I didn't—"

"Like hell. And I'm guessing you're fighting the urge to do it again."

"Just as you fought against coming over here?"

Her face burned again, at her own boldness. At the sudden spark of something close to self-hatred in his eyes. "You have no idea," he said softly, and she thought, *This can't be happening.*

Lili glanced around, but nobody seemed to be paying the least bit of attention to them. Then she met Tony's eyes again, and her stomach jumped at the way he was looking at her, as though he was being ripped apart inside.

"What's this about, Tony?"

He slightly smiled. "Beats me. Except..." He clasped her bare arm, smartly moving her through the sea of bodies and out into the yard, heavy with the scent of Aunt Magda's prized roses.

"Where are we going?"

"Over there, in the shade," he said, nodding toward the huge old oak on the other side of the yard, sheltering a sturdy tree house worn smooth from two generations' worth of kids.

Including the teenage Lili, who'd spent countless hours that summer stargazing through a million quivering leaves and giving her heated imagination its head. Now, as then, heavily flowered rhododendrons, set in a rainbow tangle of pungent marigolds and petunias, smothered the wooden fence, but the circular stone bench girding the old tree was new. She started to sit; Tony dragged her back.

"Bird poop. Better sit on the grass instead."

"And…aren't there just as many droppings in the grass?"

"Yeah, but at least you can't see them. No, wait," he said, stripping off the unbuttoned, lightweight shirt he wore over his T-shirt and chivalrously spreading it on the ground. "Grass stains are a bitch to get out of white fabric." When Lili gave him a bemused look, he shrugged, his heart-wrenching attempts at acting normal at such odds with the pain etched in his features. "At my house real men do laundry. And Daphne's made me a kick-ass expert on grass stains."

Her heart beating overtime, Lili kicked off her sandals and folded herself onto the soft cotton shirt. Tony dropped onto the grass beside her, close enough for his scent to spark the achy, bittersweet memory of unrequited longing. "Better?" he asked.

"Yes. Much. Thank you." She offered him a slight smile, then squinted back at the house. "I never have been all that comfortable around large groups of people."

"Why do you think I rescued you?"

She paused. "And not yourself?"

With a soft laugh through his nose, Tony leaned back on his elbows, his hooded gaze aimed toward the house. "Normally I'm up for these clan gatherings, but today…" His jaw clenched, he shook his head before taking a long swallow of beer. "Except no way in hell would anybody let me stray from the herd."

"So you decided we could stray together."

"Yeah. Just like old times, huh? You and me against the world."

"Is that what we were? United against everybody else?"

His mouth tilted. "Sure felt like it. I was mad as hell about my summer being screwed, you were pissed about your family dumpin' you off on Magda and Benny—"

"I was not! Especially since it was far better than the alternative."

Tony chuckled, and she smiled. She'd told him back then that, despite her father's assumption she'd join the act, by the time she was ten it was painfully obvious she had neither the talent nor the enthusiasm for the trapeze. It had taken a bit longer for the family to accept that Lili hated *everything* about circus life. Tony, however, had understood it immediately.

"Makin' you the only kid in the world who wanted to run *away* from the circus."

She shrugged. "But won't our being out here by ourselves invite…speculation?"

"Rather deal with that than the nagging. And at least this way they'll leave us *both* alone. For the moment, at least."

A breeze blew her hair into her mouth; she tugged it out, tucking it behind her ear. "Tired of being the strong one, are you?" she said quietly, not looking at him. This time when he laughed, there wasn't an ounce of humor in it.

"You always were one scary female, you know that?"

"About as scary as a newborn kitten. And you didn't answer my question."

"Not gonna, either," he said, tilting the can to his mouth again, only then seeming to notice she was empty-handed. "Hey—you want anything…?"

"No, no…I'm fine. So. Magda says you teach school?"

"Yeah," he said, his shoulders relaxing. "High school phys ed. Coach the football team." He paused. "Not exactly living the dream I had way back when. But then, how many people do?"

"You don't sound terribly unhappy about that."

"Now? No. Then…" He blew a stream of air through his lips. "That busted leg screwed up any chance I had of even making a college team, let alone a shot at the pros. So I did the next best thing and majored in PE." His mouth curved. "Smartest move I ever made." Then he sighed. "Damn, Lil— it's like no time's passed at all."

Too true, she thought, sternly telling her heart and her hormones and everything else yipping in her ears to be quiet. "I know what you mean."

"Even so…something's changed."

"It *has* been fourteen years."

"I'm not talking about the way you look. Although you look good. Maybe still a little on the reserved side, but good—"

Lili looked down at her dress. "What's wrong with what I'm wearing?"

"I didn't say anything was wrong with it, I said you looked good, didn't I? And you know that's not what I mean. There's something different about *you.* You were quiet, sure, but…why'd you take off like that, when we were talking before?"

She brought her knees up, tucking her full skirt around her legs before hugging her shins. A burst of laughter went up from the deck; Lili shooed a fly off her arm, then said, "Because I'm not sure what you want from me. It really does seem as if…as if no time's passed at all. That everything's exactly the same, even though…" Frowning, she let her eyes touch his again. "Nothing is."

Tony's eyes narrowed slightly before he made a soft, derisive sound through his nose. "I'm not sure what I want from you, either," he said, and Lili mentally stood aside to let the disappointment shuffle on through, even as she chided herself for the moment's foolish detour. Even ignoring the fact that they'd only ever been friends—for a single summer a million years ago, at that—Tony was a recent widower. One plagued by heaven knew what other issues. What on earth had she expected? A fairy tale?

"Are those your other two girls over there?" she said, steering the subject into hopefully safer territory.

Tony sat up to get a better look at the crowd, briefly bumping her shoulder. "The little curly-headed demon runnin' around with Rudy's stepsons?" he said, sagging back. "That's Daphne. She's seven, so smart I can barely keep up and gets dirtier faster than any of her boy cousins could even dream of. And the one wearing the Patriots hat and the grump face, hanging next to Stacey? That's Claire. She'll be eleven in a couple months."

"Oh, my…she's going to be a knockout, isn't she?"

"And I could have happily gone all day without you sayin' that. Although…she's been, uh, eating more since her mother died. My mother-in-law keeps making these not-so-subtle comments about Claire's diet. Like I'm gonna deny the kid the occasional bag of French fries on top of everything else she's been through?"

"Of course you're not," Lili said, her heart twisting at the obvious conflict behind his words. Not that she was any expert, but she imagined that wanting what was best for your child and wanting to make her happy weren't always compatible goals. Josie ran across the deck, not watching where she was going; Claire caught the baby as she tripped, giving her a kiss before their aunt scooped the toddler back up into her arms.

"Claire's very good with Josie, isn't she?"

"Yeah," Tony said after another moment. "She is. Bossy as hell, though. With all of us. Supposedly that's normal for the oldest kid. Especially after a loss."

"Which I suppose accounts for the frown currently aimed in our direction?"

"Don't take it personally. Claire frowns at everybody." He

sighed. "At every*thing*. What I don't get, though, is how she can be so self-assertive one moment, so insecure the next."

Without thinking, Lili laid a hand on Tony's forearm, solid as iron beneath her fingertips. "It's early days yet," she said softly, and his eyes bounced off hers.

"That's what I'm hoping."

Suddenly self-conscious, Lili folded her arms around her legs again to wiggle her bare toes in the grass at the edge of the shirt, meeting his oldest daughter's laser-bright glare from across the yard. "You're doing a good job with them. I can tell."

"Some days I'm not so sure," he said after a moment. "But nobody can say I'm not tryin' my best. My kids…they're my life, you know?"

"Obviously," Lili said, thinking, *You've grown up very nicely indeed, Tony Vaccaro.*

A thought that could make her extraordinarily sad, if she let it.

"Who's that?" Claire said, following Stacey to a couple of beat-up lawn chairs on the other side of the deck. "The woman with my dad?"

Her older cousin glanced over as she dropped into a chair. "That's Lili." She reached over her head to twist her long, shiny, dark hair up with a band so the ends all fanned out. On Stacey, it looked totally cool. Claire tried it once and looked like an alien. "Aunt Magda's niece. She's visiting for the month, I guess. From Hungary. Wouldja mind handing me a Coke from that ice chest? God, it's hot out here."

Thrilled at being asked to do something for her fourteen-year-old cousin—the rest of her older cousins usually ignored her—Claire plowed one hand through the cold, slippery cubes to get a Coke, casting a quick glance over her shoulder before sliding out one for herself, too. She'd already had one today, Dad would have kittens if he caught her with another.

Not to mention Nana, ohmigod. The chest slammed shut, Claire handed Stace her drink, then sat next to her, shifting several times before realizing no matter what she did, she was never gonna look as good as Stace, not with her stupid short legs. Or her dumb lumpy hair which never looked nice no matter what she did with it.

Being ten sucked. The older kids could do whatever they wanted, practically, and everybody loved the younger ones because they were still cute. What was super sucky, though, was being old enough to know when something was going on, but too young to do anything about it.

Claire popped the tab off the soda and glared some more at her dad and this Lili person. At least she wasn't touching him anymore, because that had just been, like, five kinds of wrong. Like she was trying to act like his girlfriend or something—

"Oh, God," Stacey said, laughing. "I know *exactly* what you're thinking. About your dad and Lili?"

Claire's cheeks warmed. "Who said I'm thinking anything?"

"Yeah, right. It's, like, so written all over your face. It's okay, I felt the same way when we first moved to New Hampshire, and Dad and Violet started making eyes at each other?" She skootched down in her chair, her eyes drifting closed. "I was all, *Get a room*—in my head, I mean—except not really, because that was so not what I wanted to happen."

When Stacey didn't say anything else, Claire squinted over at her. "But it did happen," she said, wondering if Stacey thought this was supposed to be making Claire feel better. Sweat was beginning to pop out in little drops on her upper lip. Ew. She really wanted to go back inside, but then Stacey might think she was a baby. "Violet and your dad got married."

Stacey shrugged, her eyes closed. "I got over it. But anyway, it's totally different with your dad and Lili."

"Why do you think that?"

"First off, my dad said your dad was like seriously in love with your mom. Kids are ridiculous, they break up and two days later they're with somebody else." Her eyes still closed, she did the little shuddering thing. "But grownups take for*ever* to get over a broken heart. I mean, yeesh, it took my dad, what? Twelve years? Second, they're just friends. Or were, apparently."

"Were?"

Stacey opened her eyes to peer at Claire from underneath lashes with about five coats of mascara. "Baba said Lili was here before, like before I was born. So this isn't any big whoop, it's just them catching up and stuff. Anyway," she said, snuggling back into the chair, "Lili's going back to Hungary at the end of the month. So trust me—you've got absolutely nothing to worry about."

"You sure?"

"Claire. They're, like, almost *related*. Nothing's gonna happen, okay?"

When Stacey closed her eyes again, Claire finally took a sip of her Coke. It burned her throat all the way down, making her choke so hard her eyes watered. Dad looked over, frowning, to make sure she was okay.

She waved, slipping the soda behind her so he wouldn't see.

"Is Claire all right? Should you go check on her?"

"She's fine," Tony said, finishing up his now-warm beer, trying not to react to the genuine concern in Lili's voice. Even as a kid herself, she'd been great with the younger cousins. Nice strong maternal instinct, there. "She also thinks I didn't see her drinking her second Coke of the afternoon."

"A minor offense, all things considered. And isn't it diet, anyway?"

Her accent was much lighter than his aunt's, usually, except when she got emotional. When she stopped thinking so hard about the words and let her feelings do the talking. He hadn't realized how much he'd missed it.

"Yeah, except the caffeine buzz will keep her awake half the night. Nothin' worse than a ten-year-old insomniac." He scratched his head as an icy wave of comprehension surged through him, that he sure as hell wouldn't sleep tonight, either. Or for God knew how many nights after. "Except a thirty-two-year-old one."

Lili curled to pluck at a clump of clover near her polished toes—a light pink that hardly seemed worth the bother. "So. Are you going to make good use of me or not?"

Tony jerked. "Excuse me?"

Her eyes slid to his, accompanied by a slight smile. "I'm as good a listener as I ever was. If you'd like to tell me what's really bothering you…?"

Tony sucked in a breath, both because she'd caught him off guard and because until that moment he'd had no idea how he'd *kill* to give this horrible, sick feeling inside him some air. Instead he crushed his beer can and said, "So what have you been up to for the past…what is it again? Fourteen years?" When she didn't answer, he glanced at her, then turned away again. "I can't. Not yet."

"It hurts that much?"

"Dammit, Lil—"

"Sorry," she whispered, the word as caring as a touch. And almost as devastating to his self-control. Thank God, then, she said, "I have two degrees in linguistics—I'm fluent in five languages now—"

"Impressive."

"Not really. I already spoke them when I started university—the one good thing about all that touring around Europe as a kid—but the grammar needed a bit of tidying up. So I do a lot of freelance translation work. Textbooks, novels, that sort of thing." She paused. "And I almost got married."

"Almost?" Tony said over the totally unexpected jolt to his midsection.

"Years ago. Right about the time my stepfather left my mother." She smoothed the dress's hem over her toes. "For a twenty-two-year-old."

"Ouch. When was this?"

"About five years ago."

"Damn, your mother really had it rough, didn't she? But I don't follow. What'd one have to do with the other?"

Lili tucked a long strand of hair behind her ear, a nervous gesture he remembered from before. "Mama was devastated, as you can imagine." *More than you know,* Tony thought as she added, "So it was obvious she couldn't be alone. None of the boys could take her in, since they were all still traveling with the act. So I decided to move out of the flat I'd been sharing with some university chums and back in with her until my wedding, assuming she could come live with Peter—my fiancé—and me in our flat afterward. Except Peter never really got on with my mother. The idea of our all living together, even temporarily…" Her mouth thinned. "He made me choose."

"Nice guy."

She shrugged, then said, "The ironic thing was, Mama and I had actually been estranged for a while before that. And yet when she needed me, I never even thought twice about being there for her. Because that's what you do, isn't it? When a parent or child needs you, you're there. Peter's not understanding that was a deal breaker."

"And what've you been doing since then?" When she didn't reply, Tony felt his eyebrows lift. "Cripes, Lili—you took care of your mother for five *years?*"

"Obviously I hadn't intended things to play out the way they did. Or for her to get sick. But at the beginning…" She frowned, still staring at her toes. "I'm not sure what happened, to tell you the truth. Maybe I had a delayed reaction to my own breakup, or maybe I just enjoyed getting to know my mother again, going shopping and preparing meals together, catching up on movies and books. Talking."

Her head propped in her palm, she smiled at him. "We became very good friends, during that time. Much closer than we'd been before. I honestly never felt burdened. Not even when she became ill. If anything, I was simply grateful that I could be there for her. In many ways, especially in the beginning, it felt very…safe." She sighed. "Although I suppose most people would see it as not being very brave. Which I suppose I'm not," she added with a shrug. "I mean, here I am, completely free for the first time in years, and what do I do? Come stay with my aunt and uncle for a month. How weird is that?"

"Okay, you might have a point there," he said, making her laugh, the sound deeper, richer than before. "But you know something? Screw other people. It's your life, live it the way you want to. As for you not being brave…" He shook his head. "Goin' against your family about the circus, being there for your mother, telling your fiancé to basically go take a hike…hell, Lili, you've got more guts than probably ninety percent of the people on this planet."

"You're very kind."

"Only calling it as I see it. And just for the record, that fiancé of yours was a selfish bastard who didn't deserve you. *Or* your mother."

A sudden grin lit up her eyes behind her glasses. "Spoken like someone who didn't know my mother."

"Was she anything like Magda?"

"Worse."

"Oh."

Lili chuckled, then released another breath, wrapping her arms around her legs. "Still. I feel a bit like Rip Van Winkle waking up after his very long nap, trying to figure out where I fit in this strange new world of being on my own."

Up on the deck, Uncle Benny said something that apparently cracked up their aunt, making her laugh so hard she had to lean on him to catch her breath. And the look on his uncle's face…

"You believe in love at first sight?" Tony asked out of the blue, thinking of how Benny and Magda met so many years ago, the cop falling head over heels for the circus girl after seeing her perform.

Following his gaze, Lili said, "The kind that sneaks up and surprises you? Yes, I suppose. Even though it's completely illogical."

"Not sure logic's got much to do with love."

Lili's eyes swung back to his. "Wow. Deep," she said, sending something gentle and warm and hugely dangerous snaking through him, at how easy it was, being together like this. Then he caught Claire watching them again, vibrating with worry, reminding him that nothing was easy. That being a grownup meant you couldn't just run with something because you wanted to.

His wife's apparent unfamiliarity with the concept notwithstanding.

Tony smirked. "One thing I'm not, it's deep. Just your average everything's-right-there-on-the-surface kind of guy."

"Nothing wrong with that. Still. I sometimes think the best love is the kind that happens almost effortlessly, like a plant that takes root on its own."

"Like weeds?"

She laughed again. "Like wildflowers. Certainly, there was nothing effortless about my relationship with Peter. Not that even the strongest love doesn't need tending, of course, but I should have known when it became such a struggle—" Biting her lip, she swung apologetic eyes to his. "Sorry. Don't mean to bore you with tales of my woebegone love life."

Better than mine, Tony thought, as, like a distorted St. Nicholas behind a curtain of shimmering heat waves rising from the grill, Uncle Benny called everybody to dinner. Because more than once it had occurred to Tony, too, that it wasn't right, him and Marissa having to struggle so hard to keep the flame going those last years. Sure, all marriages took work, but when every single conversation becomes a chore, you know something's wrong.

He just hadn't known how wrong, Tony thought, thinking of the letter, crushed into a drawer in his office, crushing him inside—

"Are you coming?" Lili said, already on her feet, her gaze direct and honest, her sandals dangling from one hand and the breeze blowing her hair. Tony stood, the urge to touch her— to connect with her generosity and goodness—so strong it was like an electric shock to his heart…even as he knew how unfair to both of them it would be to follow through on the impulse.

Because who was he kidding, he knew damn well what he wanted from Lili, had known from practically the minute he laid eyes on her, and it made him sick, what he was thinking. Made him realize how bad off he was, even entertaining the idea of using Lili to soothe the anger and the grief and the black, bottomless loneliness threatening to suck out his brain.

"You go on. I'll catch up later."

He wasn't at all surprised to see the confusion in her eyes. That, he could deal with. The understanding that immediately followed, however…

Damn near killed him.

All Claire wanted to do, when she saw Lili heading her way, was run. But there was no way that was happening, especially since Aunt Magda dragged her over to introduce them. When Lili held out her hand, Claire figured she didn't exactly have a lot of choice about taking it or not. At least it wasn't clammy or anything, and she didn't hang on too long, or try to hug her and act like they were going to be BFFs or something. Lili was pretty, but not like Mama. Mama was *gorgeous*—

Then she got, like, stuck in Lili's eyes, which were seriously the bluest eyes she'd ever seen, only they weren't cold like you'd expect. And her smile was just, you know, normal and stuff, not like she was *trying* to be nice or anything. So why Claire felt her face get all hot, she had no idea.

"Lili's visiting from Hungary," her aunt was saying, and Claire said, "Yeah, I know, Stacey told me," then excused herself, which she knew was rude but she couldn't help it, she felt like she was gonna cry and she didn't even know why.

Breathing hard, she ran down the deck's steps and out into the yard, toward Dad, who was sitting in the grass again with his arms folded over his knees, resting his head on them. When she sat beside him, though, he looked at her, smiling a little.

"You look like I feel," he said, and she shrugged.

"I'm okay, I guess."

Dad reached over and squeezed her shoulder. "Where's your sisters?"

"Daph's still with Violet's boys, I think. And Kevin and Julianne just got here…look," she, said, pointing to Rudy's youngest brother, laughing at Josie trying to take his eighteen-month-old daughter by the hand and lead her God knew where. Well, actually, Pip was Kevin's daughter, but Julianne's niece, except now they were married so she was Pip's mom, too. It all made Claire's head hurt.

"Pip doesn't look any too sure about going with Josie," Dad said.

"Smart kid," Claire said, and Dad actually laughed.

"I see you met Lili," he said quietly, and Claire got that tight feeling in her chest again.

"Yeah. You gonna come eat?"

"Not hungry. But you go on."

"I could bring you a burger or something—"

"That's okay, baby—"

"We could eat out here, just you 'n' me."

After a moment, Dad nodded. "Sure. That'd be cool." When Claire got up, dusting off her bottom, Dad added, "We can leave right after the cake, if that's okay."

Her eyes all stingy, Claire said, "Yeah, fine," and ran back to the deck, through all the laughter bouncing off her like hailstones.

Chapter Three

Still mulling over Tony's very obvious dismissal two hours earlier, Lili gave the kitchen sink a final rinse just as her aunt and uncle hauled in yet more leftover food from the backyard.

"Didn't I tell ya you made too much?" Uncle Benny grumbled, hefting a bowl of barely eaten potato salad—yes, the very potato salad Lili had spent an hour making—onto the kitchen table. "I keep tellin' her," he now directed to Lili as she set the sponge on the back of the sink, "nobody eats like they useta, when the boys were teenagers. And half the time, the wives are on some diet or other. Unless they're pregnant."

He said this with a pointed look for Mia, Lili's only female cousin, carting in a platter of unclaimed burgers and hot dogs. Tall and thin, her warm brown waves caught in a ponytail, Mia gave him a pointed look right back. "Jeez…nosy, much?"

"What?" Benny said when Magda swatted him. "Her and Grant, they've been married a year, already."

"Pops? They have this thing called birth control? So, you know, you can plan when you have kids?" Then she slapped her head. "What am I saying, you guys had six kids in, like, five minutes."

"Benny on baby bump watch again?" Grant said, dragging a sloshy cooler into the kitchen, and Lili was glad nobody expected her to take part in the conversation because every time she clapped eyes on the man her tongue went numb. Rich, handsome, funny—her cousin had seriously hit the jackpot. Except Lili would take an ex-jock athletic coach she could actually talk to over Mr. Adonis, any day—

Stop that.

"Like you guys don't have enough grandkids already, yeesh," Mia said, sharing a quick glance with her husband that Magda did *not* miss.

"Vat's going on?"

"Nothing, Ma," Mia said, giving her mother a huge hug, and Lili felt the sting of missing her own. "We gotta go, I got an anniversary party in the Hamptons tomorrow—"

"Oooh…" Magda's eyes lit up. "Enybody famous?"

"Nope. Just loaded. C'mon, kiddo," she said to her step-daughter, Haley, a six-year-old pixie with blond curls, as Grant embraced his mother-in-law. Mia gave Lili a hug, too, said how great it was to see her again, then they were all gone, leaving Lili alone with her aunt and uncle, their two dogs and enough food to feed Eastern Europe. For a week.

As the dogs danced around, tripping over each other, Magda surveyed the leavings, sighing. "It must be ze heat. At Thanksgiving they eat like locusts. Okay, Benny, you know ze drill. Tupperware, now, and keep it coming—" She stopped, noticing the sparkling sink and surrounding counter. "Honestly, Lili— I nefer in my life knew anyone who likes to clean like you do. My own children, zey would rather parade nekked down the street zen clean. You, I nefer even have to ask, you just do it."

Lili shrugged. "I've always liked cleaning. Putting things to rights. It's…soothing."

Magda narrowed her eyes. "You are a strange young woman," she said in Hungarian, and Benny, seated at the table, groaned.

"Aw, Mag…you know I hate when you do that."

"Hah! You remember efter we met, before I spoke English as good as I do now? How your parents vould talk in front of me, and all I could mek out was Magda zis and Magda zat. I zink zey call zis payback."

Lili laughed. "It comes from too many years living with messy brothers in tiny circus trailers. It drove me crazy. And Mama. So I'd clean while they were performing." She skimmed a finger over the clean counter. "I still like wresting order out of chaos. Not that your kitchen's chaotic—"

"Sveetheart, my *life* is chaos," she said, and Benny said, "Hey," and her aunt swooped around the kitchen table to hug him from behind. "I *embrace* chaos," she said, giving him a big kiss on his bearded cheek.

"Not me," Lili said as parts of her conversation with Tony came roaring back. "I've always avoided it at all costs." As in, her life being a series of choices based on whatever was least likely to cause her *agita*. For instance…she could have pushed Tony harder to open up about whatever was bothering him, especially when it was perfectly obvious how little she would have had to push. But did she? No—

"And yet you decided to come stay with us?" Benny said. After another ineffectual swat, Magda tugged him out of the chair and gave him a gentle shove toward the door. "What? You're throwin' me outta my own kitchen?"

"Yes. Lili and I need to talk. Voman to voman."

"Auntie—"

"And no beck-talk from you," Magda said, pointing a freshly-applied acrylic fingernail in her direction. Lili momentarily considered sliding down the drain. Especially after her aunt's heartfelt sigh, once Benny had gone.

"Ven you were here before, I was so vorried about you, zat you were—vat is zat expression? A square peg in a round hole? Ze quiet one, always vis her nose in ze books. So…" a glob of potato salad smacked into a container "—afraid of…putting yourself out zere. But I zink, is just a phase, she'll grow out of it."

Lili frowned. "Because I didn't get the circus gene?"

"Of course not, did I say that? And I couldn't be prouder of you. Five languages! And *two* degrees! But zat summer, I vatched you change from zis scared little bunny rabbit into a confident young voman—"

That was Tony, Lili thought, something sharp clutching her throat as she burped the lid over the Jell-O salad. *Tony did that to me.* For *me*—

"—only now," Magda said, "I see you and zink, vat heppened? I'll tell you vat happened—my sister let you give up your life for her—"

"But it wasn't like that! And anyway, you know as well as I do what a mess Mama was. If it hadn't been for me—"

"She vould hef put on her big girl panties and gotten on vis things! And maybe she vould hef done somezing better than just vaiting out ze last five years of her life!"

Lili frowned. "Are you implying I somehow held Mama back?"

"I'm not implying anyzing, I'm saying point-blank. And it vorked both vays. The two of you held each *other* back. For God's sake, Lili, you vere going to get married!"

Ah. "It's okay, auntie, since I eventually realized that wasn't who I needed at that point in my life. And he obviously didn't need me." She shrugged. "Mama did."

"But you were hurt."

"Of course I was hurt," she said, surprised at the twinge,

even after all this time. "It's a bitch, discovering someone isn't who you thought he was. Mama and I...I suppose we were both dealing with the same feeling of betrayal. Although obviously mine was on a much smaller scale. But it's all good now," she said, lifting her chin. "My heart's all healed. Stronger than ever, in fact."

"You zink hearts are like bones, zey're stronger for being broken?"

"Perhaps," Lili said with a slight smile. "And anyway, I believe things work out the way they're meant to. Except..."

"And how did I know there vould be an 'except'?"

The containers all filled, Lili sat at the table, frowning. "The day Mama died, I stood in the middle of the kitchen and realized I was nearly thirty and still had no more idea about what I was supposed to do with my life than I did ten years ago. Because you were right, earlier. About my not fitting in anywhere." A smile tugged at her mouth. "Ever since I was little, I was both the circus brat who didn't fit in with other 'normal' kids, as well as the oddball in the family. Now I feel as though everyone else caught the boat, leaving me stranded on the shore."

"Oh, sveetheart..." Magda sat with her, cupping Lili's cheeks in a gesture so much like her mother's Lili's eyes stung. "Trust me—zere's more zen one boat."

Lili laughed. "I certainly hope so, or I'm screwed."

Smiling, Magda folded her hands together. "So how does one go about finding one's purpose?"

"That's the part I haven't figured out yet. I suppose my translating work is useful, but it's not exactly fulfilling."

That got a thoughtful frown. "You need to be needed, yes?"

"Yes, I suppose that's it."

With a sharp nod, her aunt got up to pluck a couple of plastic grocery bags from underneath the sink, filling them with some of the storage containers. "Everybody in my femily, they tell me I'm crazy for vanting to marry somebody I barely know, somebody I can barely even talk to." The first bag filled, she started in on the second. "But efter two dates with Benny, I know he's a good man, and he needs me." After plopping in a loaf of whole grain bread some kind, misguided soul had contributed to the cause, Magda turned, smiling. "Not zat he could *tell* me. But vords...too often zey come from ze head, and not ze heart. It's what a person does zat counts, no? Who he is."

The bags filled, Magda hefted them off the counter, crossed to the table and held them out. "Don't just sit zere, get up off your skinny little butt and take zese."

"And...what am I supposed to do with them?" Lili asked, taking the bags.

"Ve can't eat all zis food, it vill go bad. Nobody else needs it, either." She grinned. "Tony, on ze ozzer hand..."

"Oh, no—" Lili tried to hand the bags back, but Magda folded her arms so she couldn't. So Lili swung them back up on the table and folded *her* arms.

"I am not going over there on some...some mission of mercy."

"And vy not?"

"You know full well vy—*why* not."

"Zen meybe you should explain to me."

"The man's just lost his wife. And Claire looks at me as if I'm carrying some flesh-eating virus. How am I doing so far?"

"You vant to be needed? I nefer see anybody needier than Tony right now."

"True. But it's not me he needs."

"I'm no so sure of zat. Lili," Magda said when Lili released a breathy laugh, "you zink I don't see the special bond you two hed before?"

"Oh, please. To Tony, I was just a little sister. An annoying one, too, no doubt."

"I am not talking about how Tony felt about *you*. But iz easy for a young girl to develop feelings for an older boy, yes? Especially a boy who treats you with such kindness?"

Lili's eyes narrowed. She'd never said one word to her aunt—or anybody else, for that matter—about her crush. That dumb, she wasn't. Even then. "Where are you going with this?"

Slowly, Madga smiled. "You remember the diary you lost, ven you were here before?"

"Yes, I…" Heat roared up her neck. "You found it."

"I might hef," Magda said, pretending to inspect her nails like some character from an old movie. "I might hef read some of it, too. Before I knew vat it was, of course. So," she said mildly, "you hef two choices. Tek the man ze demmed food, or I mek your life a liffing hell." At Lili's dumb-founded look, the older woman shrugged. "Vat ken I say, I fight dirty."

In spite of herself, Lili chuckled. And grabbed the bags' handles. Although she sincerely doubted even Magda would stoop so low as to show Tony—or anybody—the embarrass-ing ramblings of a lovesick fifteen-year-old, once again it was just easier to go with the flow. To do what was expected of her than to fight.

"Car keys?"

Her aunt dug them out of her pocket and handed them over. Smiling.

Soon after, Lili backed out of the driveway in Magda's pine-scented Ford Focus, the bags safely tucked under the passenger side dash. At the first stop sign, however, she started laughing all over again.

Because that diary? The one Magda threatened, however obliquely, to show Tony?

Completely in Hungarian.

She chuckled all the way to Tony's house.

While Josie happily batted at a flotilla of bath toys in the sudsy tub, Tony sagged against the wall between the toilet and the tub, sighing. The minute he'd walked back in the house an hour before, Fear had greeted him every bit as eagerly as the dog. And as messily. Tissues, meat trays, diapers—strewn from kitchen to front door. Although the argument between Child 1 and Child 2 about who was supposed to have put the rotten beast outside handily pushed Fear into a corner of his brain. However, unlike Ed—who at least had the good sense to cower and look guilty—Fear simply sat there, biding its time. Waiting to attack.

To pulverize him like Ed had all those meat trays.

"Hey. You 'sleep?"

"Not really," Tony said, as half smiling, he opened his eyes. Her chin propped on the rim of the shell-pink tub, Josie was watching him through water-spiked lashes like Tony was a damn miracle or something. Fear inched a little further out, teeth bared.

What if—?

"Dad!" Daphne yelled up the stairs. "Aunt Magda just pulled up in the driveway!"

Frowning, Tony scrambled to his feet, grabbing a towel off the rack. In one motion he yanked the baby out of the tepid water and wrapped her up like chubby little burrito, then tramped down the stairs. Except it wasn't Magda standing in his doorway, weighed down with bulging grocery bags, but Lili, all big eyes and soft smile and grownup curves, and he had to squelch the urge to yell *Run! Get out while you can!*

Then it occurred to him the woman was perfectly capable of fending off lunatic men with easily excitable libidos. Especially those who couldn't do anything even if they wanted to, since there were three children—

Ed woofed.

—and a dog in the house.

"Oh, my goodness," Lili said, dumping the bags to pat her thighs. Ed went nuts. *Nuts.* "Aren't you a wonderful doggy, yes, you are—no, no!" Much laughter as she tried to dodge his slobbery kisses. "What's his name?"

"Ed."

"Yes, Eddie…I love you, too—!"

"It's Lili," the ever-helpful Daphne said, looking up at him.

"I can see that," Tony said, hiking the soggy baby farther up into his arms. "Runnin' away already?"

Wiping dog spit off her chin, Lili grinned. Even if the grin did look a little undecided. "Tempting, but no. However—" she shoved Ed's head out of one of the bags to pick them up again "—she thought you might like some of party leftovers—"

"Dad? Who is it…? Oh."

"Hello, Claire," Lili said, her smile genuine but careful. At Claire's mumbled response, Tony cleared his throat and she sighed and said, "Hi, Lili," back. Not like she was overjoyed, but it was a beginning.

Except then she said, "You want me to get the baby ready for bed?" at the same time Daphne, already in her nightgown, said, "You gonna read to me tonight, or what?"

"Oh, I'm sorry," Lili said. "I didn't mean to interrupt your routine—"

"Not at all." The baby handed to Claire, Tony took the bags from Lili's hands, getting a good strong whiff of something pretty and kinda spicy which did a real number on his head— among other things—and what shreds of common sense he had left told him nothing good could come of this, even as he thought that was nuts, because there was no *this,* and wasn't gonna be.

"Come on in," he said.

Standing in the entryway with her arms crossed, Lili valiantly tried to ignore Claire's thundercloud face as Tony ducked into the kitchen, dumped the bags, then popped back out, striding over the well-worn, earth-toned braided rug.

"Coming, cupcake," he tossed up to Daphne, draped over the banister like a rag doll. Then to Lili, with a quick, nervous smile as he hooked one hand around the newel post and swung himself onto the stairs, "I'll be right back. There's soda and stuff in the fridge, if you want—" Halfway up, he pivoted to hunch over the banister. "Whatami thinking, you probably have plans or something, right?"

"Um…not really, no. But I can't stay long, I, er, promised to watch a video with Magda later." Lili nodded toward the kitchen. "I could put the food away, if you like."

"Oh. Sure. Claire, you mind showing Lili the kitchen—?"

She smiled. "Unless you moved it, I remember where the kitchen is."

"And I have to put the baby to bed, anyway," Claire said, stomping up the stairs past him, her baby sister expertly balanced on her hip. Lili watched as Tony's gaze followed them both for a second before he gave her a tight smile.

"Kids," he said, shrugging, then lightly banged his palm on the banister. "Right. Well. See ya in a few."

Ed, aka her New Best Friend, followed Lili into the kitchen, where he collapsed with a groan onto the mosaic-patterned linoleum. Underneath a pleated forehead, soulful brown eyes kept watch as she surveyed the familiar, eerily quiet room that had once been command central for Tony's large family, with Rhea Vaccaro the generous, iron-fisted general in charge of it all. The floor, dark wood cabinets and mustard-colored countertops were the same, but a huge, gleaming two-door refrigerator had usurped the old almond model, and on one rusty-red wall a trio of large paint swatches in bright, clear blues and greens hinted at changes to come.

Long overdue changes, Lili mused as she emptied the plastic bags, then tugged open one of the refrigerator doors, bringing the dog instantly to his huge feet, floppy ears perked. Eyes firmly clamped on the container in her hands, he slowly lowered his hindquarters to the floor. Looked from container to Lili to container again.

Chuckling, Lili popped it open and pulled out a hot dog. Looking as if he might weep with joy, Ed gingerly accepted the offering, only to gulp it down in a single chew—

"He's not supposed to have people food," Claire said behind her, making her jump. "It gives him really disgusting gas."

"Oh! I'm sorry," Lili said, blushing as she dove into the fridge and began rearranging innumerable deli packages, leftover Chinese take-away and half-eaten yogurts to fit in her aunt's offerings. Behind her, Ed burped, and Lili felt like slime.

Only to choke back a laugh when Claire said, "You are *so* not sleeping in my room tonight." Then, "So you were here before?"

Lili twisted around. The intense, suspicious glare was at complete odds with the girl's slouched stance, the tightly tucked arm over her round stomach, the constant twisting of a strand of hair around and around her finger. *Déjà vu,* she thought on a spike of sympathy.

"Ages ago," she said mildly, wedging containers of vinegary, red cabbage slaw and macaroni salad in amongst the chaos. Noticing that the cottage cheese sell-by date harked back to late spring, she removed it, setting it on the counter. "When this was still your grandparents' house."

"Dad's parents, you mean? They're both dead now."

"I know," Lili said with a quick, hopefully sympathetic smile. "I liked them both, very much."

"I don't really remember them. Daph wasn't even born yet."

The first batch of goodies tucked safely in their new home, Lili stood to retrieve the rest of the containers. Desperate for another conversational topic, she nodded toward the paint swatches. "I think I like the second one from the right best. How about you?"

"What?" Claire followed Lili's gaze, then seemed to realize what she was doing to her hair, perhaps because somebody had been on her case about it before. She tightly crossed her arms. "Those are from before Mom got sick. Dad hasn't had a chance to paint back over them yet."

"Paint over them? Instead of choosing one of the new colors—?"

"The red's fine. I like it."

Got it, Lili thought, plunging into the depths of the refrigerator again to shove in the hot dogs which she somehow doubted they'd ever eat. Telepathically communicating his willingness to help everyone out on that score, Ed looked up at her. And burped again.

"I suppose a new color would take some getting used to," Lili said, backing out of the fridge and shutting the door. Ed plodded off to sulk. "But sometimes it's fun to change things around, don't you think?"

"Not really," the child said with a where-do-people-come-up-with-these-things? expression. She pushed up her glasses. "Stacey says you're from Hungary, too."

"Stacey…oh, right. Rudy's daughter." *Any time now, Tony,* Lili thought as she stretched out the used plastic bags on the same pebbled glass table where she used to eat peanut butter and banana sandwiches, hand-ironing them as flat as possible before folding them into obsessively neat little squares. "That's right, I am."

"You don't sound like Aunt Magda, though."

"That's probably because I've been speaking English since I was little, whereas my aunt didn't learn it until she was already an adult."

"So how long are you staying this time?"

The words lashed across the spacious room like a whip, one wielded by a deeply wounded child still unsure of her footing in her fragile new world.

"A few weeks. I'm just here for a visit."

"Do you have a boyfriend back where you live?"

The absurdity both of the question and the situation almost made Lili laugh. And wouldn't *that* be a huge mistake? "No. I don't. Not there or anyplace else." She paused, empathizing with the fear behind the questions. The threat Lily represented to a child who'd recently lost a parent, to whom the idea of replacing that parent was far more odious than the void left in her absence. No matter how ungrounded her worries.

"Your father and I are old friends, Claire," she said gently, not surprised when the intelligent, slate-blue gaze sharpened behind her glasses. "Hardly that, even, since we haven't seen or talked to each other in so long—"

"And you're cousins, too, right? Like, family?"

"Only by marriage, not by blood. But cousins can be friends, too—"

"Ten pages," Tony said from the doorway, "and Daph was gone…" Frowning, he looked from Claire to Lili, then back to Claire. "What's going on?"

Claire pushed herself away from the counter. "Nothing. I'm going to read for a while, if that's okay."

"Sure, honey." Tony watched her leave, then turned back to Lili. "Did I miss something?"

"Only the glaring overhead light and the two-way mirror."

"What…oh." Tony sighed. "Gave you the third degree, did she?"

"Apparently my bringing leftovers set off alarms."

"Yeah, well, those alarms have hair triggers. Anything and everything sets them off these days. I'm sorry. I guess it's that protective thing kicking in again."

"So I gathered." Lili hesitated. "She reminds me a great deal of myself, after my father died. The rampant distrust, I mean."

"Didn't seem that way to me," Tony said, and she frowned at him. "Sure, you were kinda withdrawn, after you first got here. But I never felt like you were on guard or anything."

That's because I never felt I had to be on guard around you, Lili thought, saying, "I was pretty much over it by then." She nodded toward the wall. "She's having trouble with changes, I take it?"

That got a dry chuckle. "There's an understatement. I keep trying to get her to pick a color, she keeps nagging me to paint it back the way it was. Been going on for months."

"Her mother chose the colors?"

"Yeah," he breathed out. "So I thought maybe it would help, you know? Keep Marissa's spirit alive, or something." He cleared his throat; when Lili looked over, every muscle in his face had tensed. "Shows how much I know."

"Give her time." She paused. "Give *yourself* time." Feeling suddenly awkward, Lili gathered her stack of obsessively folded bags. "I should go," she said, starting out of the room, only to jump when Tony caught her arm.

"You saved my sanity that summer, Lili. I don't know if I ever told you in so many words, but you did."

She let his gaze wander in hers for several seconds before saying, "And…I suppose this might seem like a good opportunity for a repeat performance."

Tony's brows crashed over his nose. "Is that what it was? A performance?"

Oh, no, you won't, she thought, her spine tightening. If she'd held on to her self-respect as a naïve fifteen-year-old, damned if she was going to let it go now. "If by that you mean, was it a chore, keeping your company? Of course not. After all, you helped me through a bad patch, too."

He seemed to relax, if only just. "Even though it couldn't've been much fun for you. I was pretty much a pain in the ass, as I recall."

"Not any more than my brothers," she said with a smile, which he briefly returned. Lily weighed her options, skittering away like a frightened mouse ranking high on the list. But he had steered her through the worst of her grief that summer, and turning her back on him now wasn't sitting well. After all, she was only there for a few weeks, she might as well make herself useful.

"You were a good listener, too, Tony. Then, I mean—"

"Seems to me I didn't have a whole lotta choice," he said with a rueful smile. "What with my leg being in a cast and all."

"Oh, you had a choice. And I'm serious—if you need someone to talk to, I'm happy to return the favor."

"Like you don't have anything better to do than listen to a guy bitch about his sucky life?"

"Depends on the guy," she said, immediately regretting it.

Tony's eyes darkened slightly before he turned toward the refrigerator, sighing when he opened the door. "Man, FEMA would have a field day in here."

"Excuse me?"

"Never mind," he said, shutting the door again to lean heavily against it. Frowning. Obviously thinking. Then, "You ever sometimes feel like you're shoveling sand? That no matter how fast you dig, the hole just keeps filling back up?"

Fifteen years earlier Lili'd experienced firsthand the devastation the untimely death of a parent wreaks on a family.

Now, the haunted look in Tony's eyes, in Claire's, brought the memories flooding back. But she imagined Tony wasn't seeking solace as much as a sounding board. So instead of a lame, "I'm so sorry," she instead zeroed in on the practical. "Do you have help? With the house and such?"

"On a PE teacher's salary? No damn way. I mean, I manage—of course I *manage*—and the girls spend at least part of every weekend with Marissa's parents, giving me a chance to get the place cleaned up without bein' interrupted every two seconds. In fact," he said with what could only be described as guilty relief, "Susan and Lou are comin' for the girls after church tomorrow, bringin' 'em back Monday night."

"You? Clean house?" She smiled, remembering Rhea Vaccaro's telling tales on her poor, immobile son, in particular about the assorted disgusting things she'd found growing in his room over the years.

"Since it's not gonna clean itself, yeah." He rubbed the back of his neck. "Although I kinda let things slide there for a while, after the funeral. Kids got away with murder for those first few weeks, too. Well, the younger two did. Claire basically took over until her sorry father realized crawling into a corner and ignoring the rest of the world wasn't an option."

Another flash of pain crossed Tony's features before he pushed away from the refrigerator to grab a glass from the drainboard, filling it at the tap. "But I had no idea how exhausting it was, taking care of three kids, keeping track of everything they're supposed to do and doctor's appointments and…all of it. Don't get me wrong," he said, turning, "before Marissa died, I pitched in, of course I did, changing diapers and doing the shopping sometimes and folding laundry. But didn't take long to see that my 'helping out' was nothin' compared to what Marissa did, day in and day out."

"But…you were working, weren't you?"

He smirked. "Makin' a buncha teenage boys run laps or

shoot hoops isn't exactly what you'd call strenuous. Keeping three kids alive and a house off the condemned property list?" Staring blankly at some spot past Lili's shoulder, he took a long gulp of the water. "I've never been so tired in my entire life—"

"Daddy?"

They both turned to see a very sleepy Josephine toddling toward them in shortie pajamas, her blond hair all rumpled, a very strange, long-legged bird clutched in one arm. "Hey, cupcake," Tony said, immediately squatting to gather the tiny girl into his arms. "Whatcha doin' up?"

"Firsty," she said, yawning. "It's hot."

"Yeah, I know," Tony said, balancing her on his hip while he refilled the same glass he'd just used. "Daddy's really gotta do somethin' about the air conditioner, huh?"

Solemnly nodding, the toddler took a single sip of water, then shook her head. "That's 'nuff," she said, sinking against Tony's chest with her thumb plugging her mouth. Not a second later she'd fallen back to sleep. Lily smiled.

"She's absolutely precious," she whispered, not even trying to ignore all the broody feelings rising up like warm yeast inside her.

"Like this, she is," Tony said, but with such tenderness in his voice it brought tears to Lily's eyes. Then he began inching toward the door. "Well. I need to get her back to bed—"

"Yes, of course. I've stayed longer than I should have, anyway." She followed father and snoring daughter out of the kitchen, signaling to him to go on, she'd let herself out. But as she was leaving, she turned to catch Tony watching her, his gaze steady and questioning in a way that made her stomach jump. Because whatever else was, or wasn't, going on, he certainly wasn't looking at her the same way he had that summer.

Which, she thought as she stepped out into the soupy night, only made her question her sanity, that she was even considering the idea that had come to her a few minutes ago…

Chapter Four

Shortly after noon the next day, Tony opened his door to find Lili again standing on his porch, this time brandishing a mop and bucket filled with cleaning supplies, and he thought, *Please, God, no.* Ed did his happy dance and peed on the floor. In another life, Tony might have done the same thing. The happy dance, not the peeing. In this life, however…

Lili calmly dug into the bucket, ripped off a paper towel and handed it over. Tony dropped the towel on top of the pee, only to realize he was barefoot. He squatted to wipe up the mess, while Ed madly licked the air a half inch from Tony's face, sorry as all hell.

"Magda sent you again?"

"No, this time was my idea. I thought of it last night."

Tony stood, this time noticing Lili's loose, blah-looking gray T-shirt flopped over some seriously short shorts. Deep in whichever gland was responsible for noticing things like short shorts, a tiny, defiant spark erupted, momentarily obliterating the fact that, except for the girls, his life was hell on a stick.

He finally dragged his gaze back up to a smile flashing in a glowing, scrubbed-clean face behind adorably crooked glasses, and the spark cleared enough for her words to register. "Thought of what last night?"

"That while I'm here, I could help you clean the house. I assume the girls are gone?"

"Uh, yeah—"

"Good." Lili pushed past him, ponytail swishing as she and Ed headed with definite purpose toward the kitchen, one of them trailing a faint cloud of something flowery—probably not Ed—which Tony only half noticed because his gaze was glued to all that smooth, pale skin below the hem of those very, *very* short shorts.

Dude. Wrong. "What are you," he called to her back, slightly dizzy and more than a little pissed, "my own personal Merry Maid?"

"I like to clean," she said, disappearing into the kitchen. A second later, a disembodied, and apparently disappointed, "You started without me?" floated back down the hall.

Tony ambled to the kitchen doorway, where he crossed his arms across his own baggy T-shirt, worn over a pair of ancient gym shorts unfit for anyone to see who didn't share his last name. "We did eight o'clock mass, the girls were gone by ten. So, yeah. Since I had no idea you were coming. But hey, I haven't gotten to the bathrooms yet."

He could have sworn he snarled that last part. Lili, however, actually brightened, her eyes as clear and blue as the water in some tropical paradise brochure. "Wonderful!"

"Jeez, Lil—I was kidding—"

But she was already gone, mop in hand and cleaning supplies merrily rattling. Tony caught up with her at the stairs, nearly tripping over the stupid dog as he lumbered up after her two steps at a time. Not only were the legs easy on the eyes, but they moved at the speed of light. "I'm serious, I can't let you do this—"

"Oh, dear. Did you wash the dog in this tub?"

Ed lifted deeply offended eyes to Tony.

"No. Just Daph."

"How can such a little girl get so dirty?"

"It's a talent," Tony muttered, doomed, as, on a happy sigh, Lili grabbed a bottle of tub cleaner, squirted some into the tub, then dropped to her knees, sponge in hand.

"You're insane," Tony said. Now ogling her butt. Which was amazingly…round. Ed plodded over to see if he could help, but his butt wasn't nearly as interesting as Lili's.

Tony thought she might have shrugged while she scrubbed. Then she actually started humming. Transfixed, Tony dropped onto the toilet lid to watch her. She glanced up, a piece of hair snaked into her eyes. "You're not supposed to be watching, you're supposed to be cleaning, too," she said, and her damned pretty accent and damned laughing eyes and damned round butt nudged aside the self-pity he now realized he'd been clutching to him like Nonna Vaccaro that ratty black shawl she used to wear. Not a lot, not completely, but enough to see a glimmer, maybe, of pale light beyond the murky little world he'd been calling home this past year.

Then he thought of Marissa's letter and the glimmer went out.

"Already did the kitchen, remember?"

Another glance—this time, she'd apparently caught the sharpness—but she simply shrugged and turned on the squeaky old faucet. "Is there laundry, then?" she said over the water roaring into the old porcelain tub. "Or something else you need to do?"

"There's always something else that needs doing," Tony mumbled, too tired to keep up the Big Bad Ogre routine, too amazed to stay mad at her. The tub rinsed, another bottle appeared out of the depths of the Magic Bucket, this one dispensing foam all over the fixtures and tile. A little more scrubbing, a little more butt-wiggling, and shazam. Gleaming fixtures and sparkling tile.

"How'd you do that?"

"I have my ways." She flapped her hands at him. "Move."

Still seated, Tony lifted his eyes to hers. "You are not cleaning my toilet."

"Don't be ridiculous, I've been cleaning lavatories since I was seven. So go," she said, poking at him with the dry johnny mop. "You're cramping my style."

Defeated, Tony stood to leave, only to turn back when he reached the doorway, his earlier annoyance pretty much disintegrated, replaced by a gratitude so sudden and profound he nearly wept. "Thanks."

She grinned up at him from over his open toilet. "That's more like it," she said.

Two hours later, the bathrooms clean, beds stripped and changed, the living room vacuumed and dusted, Lili found Tony out in his backyard, on his hands and knees in the middle of the overgrown vegetable garden taking up half of it. The plot was nearly choked with weeds, which he was attacking as though each one was a personal insult.

"We've had so much rain, and I haven't had a chance to get out here in weeks." He straightened, removing his billed hat to wipe his forehead on the hem of his shirt, a move that revealed the midsection that time forgot. As had Lili.

"When on earth do you have time to work out?"

His shirt hem still in his hands, Tony gave her a curious look. Which is when she realized she'd said that out loud. Oops. "I lift weights a couple times a week. Try to get in a run whenever I can, if nothing else to take the edge off the stress. Hauling a two-ton toddler around doesn't hurt, either."

He bent over again to yank out another clump of weeds. "Keepin' in shape at least gives me some illusion of control, you know?"

Lili sat on the edge of the back porch, hugging her knees. "Want some help?"

"You've already done more than I should've let you. Forget it." Sitting back on his knees, he squinted over the tangled mass of vines and plants, shaking his head. "This wasn't my idea. The garden, I mean. Marissa had the green thumb, not me. But the kids wanted to keep it goin', so I said okay."

"Gardens are a lot of work."

"Tell me about it."

"I'm serious. My grandmother spent half the day during the summer in hers. It was twice the size of this one, of course, but...do the girls at least help?"

"Yeah, they do. Some. Daph more than Claire, but she does her bit, too." He tugged out a particularly vicious looking clump of weeds, tossed them aside. "This shrink or whatever we went to after Rissa died, she said it was important to keep as much continuity as possible, that it would make the transition easier. A lot of people—" he got up, moved over to a line of straggly tomato plants, weighed down with several dozen ripe fruits "—the first thing they do when somebody dies? They make a major change right away—sell the house, move someplace else, whatever. But that's like runnin' away from the grief instead of dealing with it, adjusting to life with the new hole in it. Plenty of time to make changes later. Just not right away."

He gave her a look one might have construed as a warning glance, then nodded toward the porch. "You wanna hand me that basket over there? Shoulda picked these puppies days ago."

Lili looked behind her, spying the bushel basket a few feet away. She retrieved it, the hot sun pouncing on her when she walked out into the garden. Instead of handing it to Tony, however, she began gently twisting the swollen, warm tomatoes off the plants, carefully setting them in the basket. "I see a lot of spaghetti sauce in your future."

Beside her, Tony sighed. "Actually, I'll give most of these to Magda and them. Rissa did a fair amount of canning and stuff, but it's not my thing. Here, let me take that, it must be getting pretty heavy."

As she pulled off two more tomatoes, Lili sneaked a peek at Tony's face, drawn and determined. "I hope the girls appreciate you're only doing this for them."

One corner of his mouth twitched. "Putting them first…it's my job, isn't it? If it's not good for them—" he glanced over "—it's not good, period—"

"Yo! Mister V.!" boomed from the side of the house. "I see your sorry old car sittin' out here, so I know you're home!"

"Hollis Miller?" Tony yelled back, grinning. "That you?"

A moment later, an equally grinning dark face framed in short braids appeared over the back gate. "Nobody else, Mr. V. Oh, sorry…didn't mean to crash the party—"

"Not at all…come on back! Lili Szabo," he said after the kid swung open the gate and joined them in the yard, his tall, spindly frame nearly lost inside an oversized baseball jersey and baggy pants that puddled around huge trainers, "this is Hollis Miller, one of my kids who graduated last year. Lili's sort of a cousin, visiting from Hungary for a few weeks."

White teeth gleaming in one of the most beautiful faces Lili had ever seen, Hollis extended his hand. "Pleased to meet you, Miss Szabo." Then bright, mischievous eyes flashed to Tony. "'Sort of a cousin'?"

"Her mother's sister married my father's brother."

The kid looked puzzled for a moment, then laughed, holding up his hands. "Whatever, man. Hey—my mother and me, we just moved into that new apartment complex a few blocks away," Hollis said, pointing east. "I was out getting the lay of the land when I spied that old rust bucket of yours and thought, No way, this must be Mr. V.'s place. So looks like we're neighbors." The boy turned his bright smile on Lili. "This dude saved my sorry *ass,* and that's no lie."

Tony choked out an embarrassed laugh. "I wouldn't go that far—"

"No, what you did was go above and *beyond,* man. If it hadn't've been for Mr. V.," he said again to Lili, "I probably wouldn't've even graduated, and that's the truth." He scanned the yard. "Whoa. Serious garden. In *serious* bad shape. You trying to grow your own national forest or what?"

Lili sputtered a laugh; Tony shot a brief glare in her direction, followed by a sigh. "Yeah. I know."

"Hey, man…you need some help? I usedta spend summers with my great-aunt in Virginia when I was a kid, she had a vegetable garden so pretty it'd make you cry. Anything you wanna know about vegetables and stuff, I'm your man."

Tony perked up. "Actually, that's not a bad idea. I'd be glad to pay you—"

"After everything you did for me? Forget it, helping you out's the least I can do. I gotta run now, but I got some time on Monday morning. I don't have to be at work until noon. That okay?"

"That would be great," Tony said. "In the meantime… *please* take some tomatoes and cukes off my hands. No, really," he said when the young man started to protest, "you'd be doin' me a favor."

"Mom's gonna bust something when she gets a load of these," Hollis said when Tony found another, smaller basket and loaded it up with vegetables. "She's always complaining about how those pitiful things from the grocery store taste like plastic." Basket in hand, grin firmly in place, the young man nodded to Lili, saying how nice it'd been to meet her, then strode back to the front.

"Well. It appears you now have a gardener," she said, the almost worshipful look on the boy's face now indelibly etched on her brain. "Not to mention a fan for life. What on earth did you do—?"

"Hey, we got all this stuff, and that bread you brought from Magda's...wanna stay for lunch?"

She decided he hadn't heard her. "Sure, why not?"

Compared with the blistering heat in the yard, the clean, tidy kitchen felt cool and inviting. A breeze even teased the lightweight curtains over the windows. They worked as a team to pull together their simple meal, one similar to what she might have eaten back home in her grandmother's country kitchen in northern Hungary—bread and cheese and cabbage salad, the fresh vegetables warm from the garden.

"Sorry about the air conditioning," Tony said after they took their food back outside to eat on the porch, nearly as cool as the kitchen. "Or lack thereof. My folks had central air installed when I was in college, but when it goes on the blink it's a pain in the ass to fix."

"Please don't apologize, I'm not used to it much, anyway, except at school and in public buildings. My mother's apartment got wonderful cross breezes, but even when it was still..." She shrugged, popping a piece of tomato into her mouth. "Heat doesn't bother me."

"Does anything?"

Lili frowned at him across the chipped, wrought-iron table. "What a strange question."

"Didn't mean it to be. It's just...I've never known anybody to take things as they come like you do."

Lili tore off a piece of the crusty bread. "I wasn't always that way. But with enough practice—and enough time—one can get better at anything."

"Is that why you're here now? Giving yourself time to adjust?"

"I don't know. Perhaps." She sighed. "Although it's not as if I expect to have a major revelation about what to do with my life simply because I'm here. I still have to decide what I want to be when I grow up. Where I am when that happens is immaterial."

Tony rocked back in one of the iron chairs that matched the table, his arms folded over his chest. "Any clues? About what you want to do, I mean?"

"Nary a one. But what keeps going around in my head is…shouldn't I be making a difference? Adding to the world instead of just existing in it?"

Tony looked amused. "You wanna be famous?"

She laughed. "Dear God, no. I just feel I should be doing more, somehow. Even if I don't yet know that's supposed to play out. What's so funny?"

"Hearing American slang in that accent, that's all," Tony said, looking almost halfway relaxed. "Tickles me every time."

"I watch a lot of American TV and movies, read magazines, to keep up. For my translation work? I guess a lot of it's rubbed off."

His expression suddenly pensive, Tony looked out over the garden. "For whatever it's worth…" His gaze returned to hers, giving her gooseflesh. "I'm glad you decided to come."

"You're just glad someone else cleaned your bathrooms," Lili said lightly.

"Won't argue with you there. But it's not just that." Focusing again on the garden, he brought his hands up to link them behind his head. "You make a difference, Lil," he said softly. "Just by bein' yourself."

Her face warmed. "You're embarrassing me."

"Deal with it," he said, then scratched his chin for a second before clamping his hands behind his head again. Except this time he didn't look even remotely relaxed. "Right before we came to the party yesterday? I got this letter. From Rissa, through our lawyer."

Lili felt the blood in her veins chug to a standstill. "What? But—"

"She'd apparently given it to him sometime before she died, I don't know when, it wasn't dated." He paused, a muscle clenching in his jaw. "She confessed to havin' an affair."

"Tony, no…" The dog put his head in her lap; absently, she stroked the smooth, stiff fur on his neck. "Is that what you didn't want to talk about?"

"Yeah. But it seems kinda pointless keeping secrets from somebody who's cleaned your toilets." His attempt at humor didn't even begin to mask the pain working its way to the surface. He lowered his hands. "I mean, I knew we were having problems for a while there, but…I had no idea. None. But you wanna hear the kicker?"

Although Lili braced herself, nothing prepared her for the agony that now shrieked in his eyes when he faced her. "Judging from the dates she gave? There's a good chance Josie's not mine."

Chapter Five

It had felt even better than Tony had imagined, finally giving vent to the putrid feelings inside him. But only to Lili. Because in a world where damn little was a sure thing anymore, Tony knew this about her: She wouldn't go crazy on him, and she wouldn't go blabbing to the family.

"Oh, dear God," she finally whispered. "Are you sure?"

"About the timing? Yeah. Not that there were many gaps in that department," he said bitterly, thinking how stupid he'd been, assuming because things were still more or less okay in the bedroom, they were okay otherwise. "But if she was foolin' around with somebody else at the same time..." He slammed his hand on the tabletop, making the dog jump. Lili didn't even flinch.

"Did...did she *say* the baby might not be yours?"

"Yeah. She did. I mean, sure, I'll have a test done and all but..."

Lili reached over and wrapped her hand around his. "It's going to be all right—"

"You don't know that!" Tony said, yanking free. "Nobody knows that! Especially considering the insane number of things that have gone wrong over the last year! So spare me the pats on the head, okay?"

She pulled back, her arms crossed over her ribs, but otherwise seemingly unaffected by his outburst. Tony got up to lean hard on the porch railing, the paint completely peeled off in places. Like his life, peeling away bit by bit.

"Sorry, I shouldn't've blown up on you like that."

"As you can see, I survived."

Tony almost smiled, only to blow out a harsh breath instead. "Funny how you can look back, see the clues you totally missed. We argued a lot, mostly about stupid stuff. Now I'm wondering…did Rissa feel trapped? Like maybe marriage hadn't turned out the way she thought it would?"

"In what way?"

"Damned if I knew. She'd never really come right out and say what was bugging her. Like she expected me to, I dunno, figure it out on my own. I mean…"

He turned to Lili. "I thought she understood exactly what she was getting. *Who* she was getting—a jock who wasn't gonna suddenly turn into some brainiac businessman or somethin'. Yeah, there was that time Lou—her father—suggested I come into the restaurant with him, but they couldn't've been serious about that. I mean, come on—what the hell do I know about runnin' a restaurant? Not to mention the god-awful hours. It was like I kept tellin' her—maybe teaching high school PE wouldn't exactly make me rich, but I figured the time it left me to be with the girls was a fair trade-off, right?"

"I would think so—"

"Or maybe it was this house," he said, frowning up at the sagging porch ceiling, over at the fence in dire need of repair.

"My mother left us the place when she died, all we had to pay for was the utilities and taxes. And at first Rissa said it would be fun, fixing it up. Making it ours."

He looked back at Lili. "But renovating a house like this takes big bucks, it's not like we could march into Home Depot and say, 'Make it happen.' More than once she hinted at wanting to move closer to her folks, who left Springfield about ten years ago. Closer to *Bahston*—" he deliberately exaggerated the flat accent "—to a better neighborhood."

Lili's forehead creased. "What's wrong with this neighborhood?"

"Nothing, really. But the city's been through some rough patches. Like a lot of the kids who live here…" His brow knotted as his brain switched tracks yet again. "And that was *another* sticking point. Me not wanting to leave my kids. A lot of 'em, their family life sucks, maybe school's not exactly their favorite place to be. But…"

Tony gave his head a sharp shake, feeling like a thunderstorm was brewing inside him. "But they need somebody to see past the 'tude and the bluster to the real person in there. To tell 'em, hell, yeah, they've got potential—"

"Like Hollis?"

"Yeah. Like Hollis. Like a hundred others like him, kids who know I don't take any crap off them but I respect 'em, too. Sure, there's plenty of days when my head feels like it's gonna split wide open from banging into that brick wall, when I get a kid in class I can't reach, or run into a dead-end because of some bureaucratic crap or other. It's not *fun*. But it's a helluva lot more than blowin' whistles and keepin' track of the basketballs. I mean, when they get out on that basketball court or football field—" his hands came up, fingers taut around an imaginary football "—and I see the light in their eyes, that this…this is someplace where they can forget about everything but the game, that moment, where they can just be *themselves,* white, black, Hispanic, Asian, whatever…and *damn,* that feels good."

Scratching the dog's ears, Lili smiled slightly. "I imagine so. But Marissa never understood that?"

"See, that's the thing," Tony said, dropping his hands. "I thought she did. At first, anyway. Used to be, she'd come to the kids' games, ask me how they were doing, how my day went. But I don't think she ever really got it, that what I do? It's not just a job." He dropped onto the end of an old chaise, looking out over the tangled mess of the garden. "Then she got pregnant with Josie." He blew out a humorless laugh. "That's when the bottom really fell out."

"Now you know why."

"Yeah, guess so." Leaning forward, he clasped his hands between his knees. "Although at first I just chalked it up to the pregnancy itself—after Daph, she'd made it more than clear she didn't want another kid. And I thought we'd been careful, but…" He shook his head. "Not that she wasn't okay with the girls—I mean, sure, she'd yell at 'em sometimes, name me a mom who doesn't—but me? Unless it was to talk about the house or the kids, I might as well not have existed." He scraped a hand across his jaw. "Crappiest nine months of my life."

"And let me guess. Nobody knew."

"Are you kiddin'? After everything we went through to convince our parents we weren't making a mistake getting married so young? No damn way. Even so, I said I'd go to counseling, whatever she wanted. No dice. Frankly, I was worried maybe she even wouldn't bond with the baby. But whaddya know—soon as Josie was born, it was like the old Marissa was back. Acted no different with Josie than she had with the first two. Cuddled with her just as much, always right there if she so much as made a peep…"

He felt his eyes sting. "She was a great mom. Whatever

problems the two of us might've had—no matter what I know now—nothing can change that. And anyway, after the baby came…she started acting like she wanted to make things up to me, even though of course I no idea that's what she was doing. Then…"

He ground one fist into his palm. "Then she got sick. Just when it looked like maybe we could get things back on track. Went through her like wildfire. Chemo, radiation—nothing even made a dent. Although…this is gonna sound crazy, but—"

"What?" Lili said gently.

"It was almost like she didn't *want* to fight it. Like…like the guilt was literally eatin' her up. The thing is, if I'd've known, if she'd've just come out and told me, maybe we couldn've worked through it somehow."

"Do you really think that would have made a difference?" Lili said, even more gently. "In the outcome?"

"Judging from what she wrote me? I think she died in the kind of pain that has nothin' to do with the body."

Lili frowned slightly, then got up and walked to the porch railing. "And now she's passed that guilt on to you."

Tony's head jerked up. "What? No—"

"I know you're not asking for advice," she said, turning. "As if I'd have anything to offer on that score. But why are you taking so much of this on yourself? Yes, of course it takes two to make a relationship work, and it takes two to make it fall apart. But your wife's having an affair…" Her eyes sparked. "That wasn't your fault. And for *God's* sake, neither was her death."

His mouth twisted. "You think I sound off my nut?"

"No. You sound like someone trying to make sense out of something that makes no sense whatsoever. Only sometimes…things simply *don't* make sense. And all the mental juggling in the world won't change that."

A long, ragged breath left his lungs. "But all these thoughts…they're battering the hell outta me, Lil. First I'll think Josie looks exactly like Claire did at that age, she *feels* like my kid, whatever the hell that means. The next minute I'm scared to death I'm gonna answer the door one day to find some dude standing there, demanding his daughter. Except then I think it's been too long, if somebody else is the father, maybe he never knew. Maybe Rissa never told him, because *she* didn't know. She didn't go into details, for all I know maybe it was a one-time fling. Or…or maybe it wasn't, maybe she'd planned on leaving me, but her getting pregnant was a deal breaker with the other guy. Then I think, dear God—if Josie's not mine, do I tell her? When? And Marissa's parents…how on earth do I tell them—"

"Tony, Tony…" Lili crossed to kneel in front of him, taking his hands in both of hers and pulling him into those damn eyes of hers again. "For God's sake, you're going to make *yourself* sick with all this worrying and wondering. Have the test done, as soon as possible. Then figure out what comes next. But all this conjecturing is pointless."

"Maybe I don't see it as pointless," he said flatly. "Maybe I see it as bein' prepared for the worst. I've been raising that little girl virtually on my own for the past year," he said through a thick throat. "That feeling you get when you see the baby for the first time, and they reach right in and grab your heart… You think I'm gonna suddenly love her less if I find out my blood's not in her veins?"

"No. Of course not."

Tony's eyes dropped to their linked hands as the stupid dog came over to flop on his back, hoping for a tummy rub. "It would kill me, losing Josie. Losing any of 'em."

Her eyes followed his. She let go, like she suddenly realized what she was doing, then stood. "Just as it killed you to lose Marissa?"

Palming his head, Tony said, "I just wish I knew what went wrong. It's like there's this hole inside me where the answered questions should be." He lifted his eyes to Lili. "Only there's nothin' to fill it up."

To avoid those tortured eyes, Lili squatted again to pat Ed's stomach, the sense of déjà vu so strong it nearly made her dizzy. Memories of Tony's lying on that very chaise fourteen summers ago, his leg immobile as they talked about whatever crossed their minds; her mother's nearly identical laments, after Leo's betrayal—the recriminations, the transferred guilt, the lot. And hadn't she berated herself for months, after Peter so cavalierly shrugged and walked away from their two years together, certain *she'd* been the flawed one, somehow?

She supposed there were two kinds of people in the world—those who believed nothing was their fault, and those who believed everything was. How odd, when it was obvious that things were rarely that cut-and-dried.

"Swear to God," Tony said with a soft, deprecating laugh, "I had no idea that was all gonna come out. But you being here…in some ways it's like being in a time warp. Even then, I felt like I could talk to you in a way I couldn't to anybody else."

Lili forced herself to catch his embarrassed smile in the porch's shadow, not sure what she felt when he looked at him. Sympathy, she supposed, mixed in with a little irritation. Then she thought of his expression when he talked about his students, his obvious pride in Hollis, and her stomach free fell. She did her best to smile back.

"So everything's the same between us as it was then?"

Their gazes held for several seconds before Tony stood, eventually going down the steps to the netted cherry tree close to the house, ablaze with clusters of bright red fruit. "Whaddya think—these look ripe to you yet?"

For a moment Lili felt as though she'd picked up the wrong

book, confused because she couldn't find where she'd left off. But she finally joined him, pulling a firm, warm fruit off the tree and popping it into her mouth.

"Not yet," she said, making a face as the sour juice exploded over her tongue. "Another week or so, I think."

"You nut," Tony said softly. "You didn't hafta do that."

"What's life without a little risk?" she said, spitting out the pit.

He turned away again, the hot, heavy breeze ruffling his already messy hair. "So you can't feel it?"

"Feel what?"

His eyes found hers again. "That of course it's not the same between us. How could it be? We're not the same people we were then."

The knotty, sturdy tree trunk poked between her shoulder blades when she leaned against it, her hands tucked behind her back, the shade a welcome relief from the searing heat. Except, this close to Tony, *relief* was a relative term.

"Perhaps we're not so very different," she said. "Not at heart. For instance, I see the same person I did that summer. Just one who's been tried and tested."

Tony palmed the trunk, barely six inches over Lili's head, his earnest, direct gaze sending a chill through her. "How come you never returned my e-mails? And don't tell me you didn't have the Internet then, because Aunt Magda told me you'd write to her from your library's connection."

Lili pushed herself away from the tree. "What would have been the point?" she murmured, gasping when he caught her arm.

"The point is, I thought we were friends. When you left...I missed that. Missed you."

A strand of hair tumbled free of the elastic band holding it back; she jerked it behind her ear. "Did Marissa know you were e-mailing me?"

Letting go, Tony frowned slightly. "What does that hafta do with anything?"

"Did she?"

"I dunno. Maybe. Why?"

Lili hesitated, then said, "It turned out my mother's main reason for sending me away that summer was so she could marry Leo. Without it 'upsetting' me."

"What does that have to do with—?" At her sharp look, he lifted his hands and went with the flow. "But I thought your dad had just died?"

"Not even six months before, to be precise." Lili's mouth flattened. "I'd met Leo exactly once, for about five minutes."

Tony swore. "And how did she think keepin' it a secret *wouldn't* upset you?"

"I doubt she was *thinking* much at all, to be blunt. Being on her own—being alone—petrified her. Obviously. To the point where she was more than willing to let someone else do the thinking for her. She told me later the quick marriage had been Leo's idea."

"This is same jerk who dumped her, right?"

"Yes. And no, the irony was not lost on her. But my point is…I was still reeling that summer. Which you know. To come home and discover my mother had betrayed my father's memory…"

"Your father, hell," Tony said softly, pulling her into his arms. Startling the life out of her. "She betrayed *you*. Damn, honey…I can't imagine how rough that must've been for you."

Tears welling in Lili's eyes as she settled against his chest, her hands curled underneath her chin. "It felt worse than the grief," she said after a moment. "In fact, I was so upset that I went to live with my grandmother, because I couldn't bear to be around my mother and *him*. In any case, I was so wrapped up in feeling sorry for myself that my time here didn't even feel real." *You didn't feel real.* Blinking, she pulled away, lifting her eyes to his. "I read the first few e-mails, but they felt as though they'd been written to someone else. After a while I marked them as 'read' and moved on." She shrugged. "I'm sorry."

"Yeah. Me, too." At the edge to his voice, she frowned. "Dammit, Lil—you should've talked to me. Told me what was goin' on, what you were feeling—"

"And what could you have possibly done?"

"Listened."

And he would have, she thought, in a way nobody else ever had. Even now, twisted up in his own problems as he was, his umbrage on her behalf for something that had happened half a lifetime ago vibrated from him like an aura. The man *cared* about other people with a bone-deep sincerity that could make a girl fall in love with him, if she weren't careful.

Lili reached up to place a quick, light kiss on Tony's rough cheek, breathing in the scents of dark, damp earth and sweat, the soap he'd washed up with before lunch. "I somehow doubt Marissa would have been okay with that," she whispered, then walked away. But when she reached the porch, she turned back. "If you like, I could come back again next weekend. To help you clean?"

His gaze burned into hers, dark and troubled and smoldering with something even she had no trouble recognizing. Something that, if she had a grain of sense, would make her rescind her offer on the spot. "You really are nuts," he said, barely smiling.

"Then I'm in good company."

His chuckle followed her all the way back to her aunt's.

Tuesday morning, ten a.m. Vibrating with suspicion, Claire yanked back the kitchen curtain, her backpack thudding to the floor. "Who the heck is that?"

Tony's in-laws had just dropped the girls off, after begging to keep them an extra day. The garden turning out to be, according to Hollis, an inch away from hopeless, the kid had returned early that morning to continue his mission. Right now that meant battling Ed for the remaining ripe tomatoes. Judging from the kid's periodic shouts, the dog was winning. Dog really would eat anything.

"That's Hollis," Tony said mildly, his arms full of Josie, his head full of Lili. Like it had been all weekend. If he'd thought the path he'd been headed down before had been dangerous, this was a one-way road to hell. The odd kick to the groin, he could handle. That was…reflex. Hormones. Annoying, but easily dismissed. Okay, maybe not that easily, but at least manageable—

"He usedta be one of my students. Now he's our gardener. Sort of."

The kick to the center of his chest, though… Uh, boy. That was bad news. Really bad news. The kind of bad news you can't forget even after you change the channel—

"We have a *gardener?*" Daphne said, giving Tony raised brows. "Like Nana and Gramps have a gardener?"

"Not exactly," Tony said. To air, as it happened, since the child had already disappeared to accost the unsuspecting young man currently trying to tame their cantaloupe vine before it ate the neighbor's children.

"Daph!" Claire yelled out the window. Like that was gonna do any good.

Tony laid a hand on her shoulder. "It's okay, honey. If anything, Hollis should be afraid of Daph—"

"Why do we need help with the garden?"

"Because Mom's not here, and I suck at gardening, and you guys are too young to keep it up. You want a garden? Hollis is part of the deal."

Claire shot him a wounded look, grabbed her backpack

and stomped out of the room. "And he's staying for lunch, too!" Tony yelled in her wake, because he could.

Then he immediately felt like a bum for yelling at his kid, so he tramped upstairs after her, Josie giggling as they bounced up each step. Claire was sitting on her bed—legs crossed, elbows jammed on knees, scowl firmly in place—on some cutsie cartoon character bedspread which she refused to give up, despite both its threadbare state and her seven-year-old sister's declaration that it was for "infants." But at five, Claire had said she wanted a pink room; Marissa had obliged her with the pinkest room in the history of little girls. Pink, and frilly, and so intensely girlyfied Tony felt like Shrek every time he walked in.

"So how was it at Nana's?"

Claire shrugged. "She taught Daphne the breaststroke."

"What about you?"

"I already know the breaststroke."

"No, I mean, did you swim?"

"Yeah. But only because if I hadn't, Nana would've been totally on my case—Was everything all right? Was I feeling okay?" She shrugged again. "So I swam."

"You usedta love swimming."

"It's not much fun anymore."

"Because…Mom's not around to swim with you?"

"I guess."

Josie crawled off Tony's lap and over to her sister to pat Claire's shoulder. "Don't be sad, C'are," she said, practically twisting herself upside down to see Claire's face. "It's okay." With a wobbly smile, Claire pulled Josie into her lap, resting her cheek on top of her sister's head.

Tony forced air into his lungs—somehow he was gonna have to find a way to get that DNA test done soon, before he lost his mind altogether. But it wasn't like he could take everybody with him to the testing place, or leave the girls with somebody and take JoJo without it looking weird—

"Dad? What's wrong?"

"Nothing, honey. Just got a lot on my mind."

"Like what?"

"Like…I was just thinking about…how nobody likes change. But it happens anyway. And even when it seems like our own world has come to a grinding halt…" He reached over to push her hair away from her face. "The rest of the world keeps chugging along. The longer we sit around, cryin' in our beer about how we wish things were the same…" He shook his head. "The more we get left behind."

Her eyes lowered, Claire picked at a loose thread in the bedspread's quilting. "I know that," she said quietly, then lifted watery eyes to his. "It's just…it's like every time I turn around, something *else* is different. And I feel like I can't keep up."

"Yeah," Tony said, thinking about the last few days, about Marissa's bombshell and Lili's reappearance and the five million mixed-up thoughts zooming around and around his brain like one of those insane motorcyclists in the cage at the circus. "I know what you mean."

When Josie crawled off her big sister's lap, and then the bed, to pull one of Claire's old books off her shelf, Claire reached for a bedraggled Clifford the Big Red Dog Tony had brought home for her before she was born.

He half smiled. "Bet you don't remember how you useta say his whole name, every time, when you were little."

"I still do," Claire said, her own lips tilting slightly.

"So you still have Clifford," he said, "And we're still living in the same house. And school's the same, so you've got all your friends, right?"

"Yeah," she said, hugging the dog. "And…I've still got you and Daph and Ed and JoJo…" She looked up at him. "I guess lots of stuff's still the same, huh?"

"So, see? There ya go."

The shabby toy returned to its place of honor in the center of her pillows, Claire leaned against Tony as Josie "read" *One Fish, Two Fish* at their feet. "Feel better?" he said softly into her tickly hair.

She nodded, then leaned back, her expression dead serious. "Just promise me something."

"And what's that?"

"*Please* don't get married again."

"Not planning on it," Tony said, even as the feel of Lili's lips grazing his cheek scooted through his brain.

And kept on going.

Chapter Six

"Hot damn," Lili heard behind her when Hollis came in through the back door the following Saturday afternoon. "You got some *serious* cleaning mojo! Hey, Mr. V.!" he yelled down the hall. "Come see what this woman did to your kitchen!"

"For heaven's sake, Hollis," Lili said, peeling off her rubber gloves. "It's not that big a deal." Although she had to admit surveying her handiwork definitely gave her a warm, bubbly feeling inside. Something she'd tried, in vain, to explain that morning to her aunt, who eventually tossed up her hands and clack-clacked away on her spindly heeled mules, muttering in Hungarian.

Hollis snorted. "I usedta think my mother was the Queen of Clean, but this puts her to shame. Although you did not hear that from me—"

"Holy cow."

Tony's words provoked another sort of warm, bubbly

feeling entirely. The kind that came from sharing chores with a man who had no clue how good he looked in a sleeveless sweatshirt. One whose smile took some coaxing these days to come out of hiding, but, oh, was it worth the effort. Tony walked past her to the stove, all bulging shoulders and hard calves, to run a finger along the metal strip edging the cooktop. "How did you *do* that?"

Lili shrugged, pleased at the oblique compliment. "What can I say, dirt quakes in my presence."

The smile came out and Lili lost her breath. "Obviously. Damn, you're amazing," he said, and their gazes locked, and her heart sort of seized up, until Hollis cleared his throat, breaking the spell.

"I should go," she said, grabbing her cleaning bucket, and Tony said, "Actually, why don't you both stay for dinner, since it's so late? Marissa's parents should be back with the kids in about an hour, I could do burgers on the grill or something."

"Sorry, man," Hollis said, "but Mom's got people coming around, I gotta stop by the store and pick up some stuff. So later, yo. Tell Daph to keep an eye on the cukes." Grinning, he let himself out the back door, and Tony turned to Lili.

"So that leaves you."

"No, it doesn't. For many reasons. Not the least of which is that I've been vanquishing grease harking back to the mid-nineties all day—"

"Hey!"

"—so I'm sweaty and my hair's a wreck and I smell funny. Hardly fit to meet your in-laws."

"So go get cleaned up. Like I said, you've got an hour."

Rolling her eyes, she started for the door. "And how come the kids are coming back tonight, anyway? I thought their grandparents kept them through Sunday."

"They got plans for tomorrow or something, I didn't get

all the details." He gently clasped her shoulder, making her turn. Making her fall into those earnest eyes. "I'd really like you to come for dinner."

"To…what? Run interference?"

"Hardly. I can handle my in-laws, believe me. But I'd like them to meet you. What?" he said at her headshake. "We're all family, right?"

"I'm not sure they'd see it that way. And what if they get the wrong idea?"

Comprehension flitted across his features before, sighing, he crossed his arms over his chest. "You know, I spend my entire life bendin' over backward to make everybody happy. And that's fine, that's my job. But every once in a while, I like to do something for *me*. Like watch a movie nobody else wants to see. Eat a whole bucket of hot wings by myself." Lili laughed, and Tony smiled, although it wasn't nearly enough to dispel the cloud darkening his eyes. "It's the little things that keep you sane, you know? And right now, what I want is for you to let me feed you. To say thanks for demolishing twenty years' worth of grease from that stove. Is that too much to ask?"

You have no idea, she thought, even as she said, "Of course not. Except…this isn't really about thanking me for cleaning, is it?"

His nostrils flared when he sucked in a breath. "Problem with manual labor, it gives you far too much time to think. Especially when you've got a lot to think about." He paused. "Okay, maybe I could use the moral support."

"Now was that so hard to admit?" she said, smiling.

The look he gave her sent her scooting out the door.

A half hour later—showered, dressed and mentally bolstered—Lili let herself in through the partially open front door, following the throbbing rock music to the den at the back of the house, where Tony sat in an old leather recliner with a beer in his hand and the dog at his feet. The dog leaped up—*Ohmigod, you're back!*—his greeting much more enthusiastic than Tony's, who barely grumbled a "Down, you stupid mutt" as he stared at the empty fireplace.

Divested of crazed dog, Lili perched on an ottoman near the hearth. "Let me guess," she shouted over the noise. "You've been thinking again."

"One of the hazards of havin' a brain." Tony aimed the remote at the CD player to lower the volume before looking at her, his expression misleadingly blank. He, too, had scrubbed up, now wearing jeans and a clean T-shirt spouting some witticism, his bare feet shoved into a pair of well-worn moccasins. His gaze flicked over her before a small smile curved his lips. "You flyin' blind tonight?"

"Contacts. I don't wear them much. They bug."

"S'okay, you look good in glasses." He hoisted the beer can in her direction. "I like your hair like that. The dress, too. Nice color."

Lili reached up to touch her hair, quickly piled on top of her head. The dress, though, was nothing special, just some bland, bomb-proof jersey number that traveled well. In a blue that made her eyes brighter.

"Thanks," she said as Tony tilted the beer can to his mouth, muttering, "I'm a jerk," after he swallowed.

"Oh, dear," she said, making him frown at her. "Are you drunk?"

Chuckling, he shook his head. "From one beer? No."

"Then why do you think you're a jerk?"

The smile died as he stared at the hearth. "Because I'm taking advantage of your good nature."

Lili poked his ankle with her toe, getting another frown for her efforts. Tough. "I'm not a pushover, Tony. I make my own choices. If I really hadn't wanted to accept your invitation, I wouldn't have."

Another nod preceded his collapsing back into the chair. "Good to know. Still. I don't wanna come across as some sonuvabitch user."

"Not possible." Grabbing his hand, Lily dragged him to his feet. "Especially since you promised me food."

But when she tried to let go, he held fast. "This is just like before, isn't it? You not letting me wallow."

"I don't let *anybody* wallow. Wallowing only gets you stuck in the mud. Look, I hurt for you, for what's happened. And I'm angry for you, too. But I'd like to think I can be there for people without—what's that you Yanks call it? Enabling them?"

His gaze rested in hers for a moment before he headed toward the kitchen, not speaking until he'd yanked a package of frozen hamburger patties out of the freezer compartment and thunked them onto the counter. Then he leaned heavily on the edge, shaking his head. "I've been thinkin' about what you said, about how sometimes things just don't make sense, but…" He pulled out a knife five times larger than he needed to pry apart the patties. "It just won't let go, Lil. That all the signs were *right* there in front of me, and I totally missed 'em."

"And *I* repeat—that wasn't your fault."

"It is—" he whacked the first two burgers apart "—if you've got your head so far up your ass—" and the next ones "—you think as long as nobody's actually fighting?" He jabbed the knife between the last two patties so hard one went skittering across the counter. "It's all good."

Still brandishing the knife, Tony shut his eyes, breathing hard. Lili gently pried the potential weapon from his hands, setting it far out of reach before wrapping her arms around this strong, macho man who was hurting so badly and had no earthly clue what to do about it. Not surprisingly, he shrugged her off.

"I'm fine, I'm…" He retrieved the errant patty and

dumped it back on the plate with its friends. "I *loved* her, Lili. And I had no clue. None." His tortured gaze cut to hers. "And what I really can't figure out is if she didn't see fit to tell me at the time what was goin' on, why the *hell* did she bother tellin' me at all? And why so long after her death?"

"I don't know," Lili said, even though she knew he didn't really expect an answer. And it had still only been a matter of days since Marissa's bombshell; the endless whys had plagued her mother for literally years—an experience that, if nothing else, had taught Lili patience.

Which was partly why she hadn't pressed Tony about the DNA test. After all, there was no guarantee the result would be in his favor; she couldn't imagine how terrifying that prospect might be. In his shoes, she'd probably be dragging her heels, too.

"But while you're trying to figure it all out," she said, picking up the platter of frozen burgers, "at least you're not going through it alone."

His eyes grazed hers. "For as long as you're here, anyway. Right?"

"Right," she said over the sudden, sharp ache in her chest when he smiled.

A breeze cooler than Tony might've expected wicked the moisture from his skin, carried the grill's charred-beef-scented smoke into neighboring yards. He flipped the burgers, annoyed that it was a perfect summer evening, thick with the roar of lawnmowers and whine of weed whackers, with kids' clear, high shouts as they splashed in above-ground pools or kicked a soccer ball in the street. The kind of evening where you'd sit out and smell the sweet, rich scents of honeysuckle and newly cut grass as you watched giggling kids chasing fireflies….

He rubbed a wrist across his own eyes, stinging from a sudden barbecue backdraft. Or so he told himself, his thoughts knotted up inside his head like a Twister game gone bad. Like it wasn't bad enough that the night reminded him of a hundred others, of him and Rissa sitting on that porch, feeling the breeze and smelling the honeysuckle running riot along the back fence and laughing at the kids. Then he had to invite Lili over, on top of it? To what? Hold his hand?

Yeah, chalk that one up to a brain fart of epic proportions.

He started slightly when she nudged his arm, handing him an thermal tumbler of something with ice in it. "Lemonade," she said, sitting on the arm of an Adirondack chair Rissa had bought at some end of season sale. "I found a can of concentrate in the freezer."

"Thanks," Tony mumbled, taking a sip, shuddering from the tartness. Not looking at her. Lili'd made herself scarce, once he'd put the burgers on. God only knew what she'd been up to.

She cleared her throat. "When do you expect the girls?"

"Any minute…actually," he said at the sound of a car pulling up out front, "I think that's them now." He looked into those steady blue eyes, even bigger without her glasses. "You ready for this?"

"As I'll ever be," she said, standing and smoothing her hand over her dress just as

Daph barreled out the back door to wrap her arms around Tony's hips. "Burgers! Yes!!!" she chirped, as one by one, everybody else drifted out. Or, in Susan's case, floated, in a soft, crinkly skirt that brushed her ankles and a neat white top pulled in at the waist with one of those silver Native American belts. And lumbering behind came Lou, his father-in-law, in a designer golf shirt that was too bright, flashing a genuine Rolex that was too big, even on Lou's beefy wrist.

Catching sight of Lili, Josie inexplicably ran toward her— jeez, she'd only seen Lili once, twice at the most—hands raised. Lili eagerly obliged, swinging his little girl into her arms and hugging her with a gentle fierceness that stabbed Tony right in the gut.

As expected, his in-laws' expressions weren't a whole lot different from Claire's, the child giving Tony a "What the hell?" look that might've been funny on somebody else's kid. Although he had to hand it to Susan, the woman was a master at hiding what she was really thinking—she didn't need no stinkin' Botox to keep her face frozen when it suited her purpose.

"Go wash your hands, guys," he said in a low voice, smiling for Rissa's parents after the kids ran, shuffled or toddled off. "Susan, Lou," Tony said, pissed that they were jumping to conclusions, even more pissed that maybe they weren't jumping all that far. "This is Lili Szabo, Magda's niece from Hungary. She's staying with Magda and Benny for a few weeks. Lili—Lou and Susan Pellegrino. Marissa's parents."

Without missing a beat, Lili stepped forward to pull an obviously startled Susan into a hug. "It's so lovely to meet you," she said, letting go to include Lou in her gaze. "Although I'm so sorry to hear about your daughter. My deepest sympathies."

Marissa's mother pressed one hand to her chest, the white-tipped fingernails shiny and square and as perfectly even as her teeth, bared in a smile so stiff it had to hurt. "Thank you, Lili, that's very sweet. And it's nice to meet you, too." To be fair, Tony had seen plenty of genuine smiles from the old gal over the years. This wasn't one of them. "Claire was telling us all about you." Her gaze swung to Tony's. "That you two knew each other from before?"

"A long time ago," Lili said smoothly. "We weren't much more than children. I wasn't, at any rate. Um…the hamburgers are nearly finished—why don't you stay for dinner with us and the girls?"

The smile still in place, Susan's eyes smoothly slid to

Tony's, underneath short blond hair that swear to God hadn't budged since his and Rissa's wedding. "Is the meat freshly ground? And lean?" She glanced in Claire's direction, then lowered her voice. "Because some of us are watching our weight, you know."

Tony let the prickle of irritation play on through before he said, "I suppose it was freshly ground before they froze it. Lean I don't know about. But they're skinny, does that count?"

Judging from the flicker in those bland gray eyes, she got the message. "Of course it does, sweetheart. And I know how hard it must be on you, trying to make sure *every* meal's nutritious—"

"Tony made a salad, too," Lili said, taking the woman by the arm and steering her back toward the kitchen, and Tony wondered what "he'd" made it out of, exactly, since it'd been a while since he'd hit up the produce aisle. Yeah, they had tomatoes and cukes out the wazoo, but the leafy green stuff might be kinda iffy. As he transferred the charred excuses for hamburgers to a paper plate, Lou came up beside him, blessing the world at large with his cologne. Even so, Tony'd always liked his father-in-law, the son of a factory worker who—the Rolex notwithstanding—was still just an average Joe from the old neighborhood who'd done good.

"Those look great," he now said, and Tony laughed.

"You gotta be kiddin' me? You own one of the best restaurants in Boston, and you're salivatin' over a bunch of burnt, pre-pressed burgers?"

The older man shrugged, his hands in his khakis pockets. "Reminds me of when I was a kid. Bad burgers, rubbery hot dogs, hot off the grill—now *that* was summer. These days it's salmon and chicken breasts and grilled vegetables. That's not summer, it's hell."

"Susan's just watching out for you. Making sure you eat right so you'll be around for a long, long time."

"Killin' me with kindness, is what she's doin'," Lou grumbled, but with a *yeah, you're right* shrug and grin.

Maybe Susan went overboard with the worrying, and maybe Lou sometimes flashed his success more than Tony might've liked, but at heart they were good people. Good people who'd defied *their* parents when they'd fallen in love and wanted to get married, good people who were still devoted as hell to each other after more than thirty years. Finding out Marissa had cheated on Tony would be like a stake to the heart. If Josie ended up not being his...

Tony pulled a hamburger bun out of the package and plopped it on a plate. "Here. You get dibs."

"Yeah?" The older man surveyed the plate, then said, "You pick. But you got enough to stick two patties on there? Just for God's sake don't tell Suze, she'll make me eat bean sprouts for a week. Yeah, like that. You got mustard? Ketchup?"

"Over on the table. So I take it the girls didn't give you any trouble?"

"You kiddin'?" Lou said, pumping the ketchup bottle. "They're angels, all three of 'em. Although JoJo..." Chuckling, he smothered the burger with ketchup, then went for the mustard. "She's somethin' else. Knows exactly what she wants and goes after it. Doesn't take 'no' for an answer, either. Just like her mother. You got pickles?"

"In the fridge."

"Forget it, then."

"I should call the kids—"

"No, wait a sec, I wanna talk to you." Lou smashed the top half of the bun over the burger, sending mustard and ketchup squirting out the sides, before taking a seat at the table and looking out at the girls, now back outside. Daphne and Josie were playing ball with Ed—so much for the clean hands— while Claire sat listlessly on one of the swing seats, keeping an eagle eye on her sisters.

"That one's got the world on her shoulders, doesn't she?" Lou said softly before taking an enormous bite of his burger. "Since her mother died, I mean." At that moment, the dog accidentally knocked the baby over. Even though she was obviously unhurt, Claire was instantly on her feet, pulling Josie to her and giving the dog hell. "See what I mean?"

"Actually," Tony said, on guard, "she was like that before. Kid was born with the mother hen gene."

"True. But you know what I'm talkin' about, right?"

Yeah, he knew. That Lou was about to bring up a subject Tony had fervently hoped they'd buried along with Marissa, after Lou had taken Tony aside and expressed concern about how Tony would be able to take care of three kids on his own. "Lou, don't."

"What? Try to make you see reason? I got a good manager for the restaurant now, I hardly ever go in, maybe once, twice a week. Suze and me, we got more time on our hands than we know what to do with—"

"Then travel, for God's sake," Tony said. "Go build houses for Habitat for Humanity. Join a swinging singles club, I don't care—you're not getting my girls." Trying to control his breathing—and his voice, since he didn't want the girls to hear—he added, "I know you and Susan had issues with Marissa marrying me to begin with, that you never thought I was good enough for her—"

"That's not true, Tony, and you know it." At Tony's lifted brows, Lou sighed. "Okay, so maybe it bothered us, at the beginning, that Rissa didn't really understand what she was getting into. The two of you were so damn young, Tony—of course we were gonna worry. But it had nothin' to do with you, I swear. And anyway, you proved us wrong. When I saw how you were suffering, when Rissa got sick…"

Lou looked away. "We're not talking about taking 'em from you, Tone. Just…helping out. Until they're a little older, a little easier to take care of. In the meantime, there's this good private school, just down the road from us—"

"The kids are fine where they are, Lou. They're fine *here*. I know…I know how hard this has been on you, Rissa being your only kid. But you can't have mine."

Finally, the old boy nodded. "Exactly what I told Suze you'd say. If that's how you feel…" He lifted his hands. "Then that's how you feel."

Right. Like Tony didn't damn well know that while Lou might be conceding the battle, the war was far from over. But nobody was getting his girls, he thought, watching Josie throw her arms around Ed's neck and give him a great big kiss on the snout.

Nobody.

"That's better," Susan said, returning to the kitchen from the downstairs bath after she'd gone to "tidy up." Seething from the exchange she'd just witnessed through the kitchen window, Lili watched her cross to the counter, where she'd left her large, obviously expensive designer bag, to fish out a tube of obviously expensive designer lotion, which she then squirted into the palm of one hand. "Sorry I took so long, but that sink looked as though it hadn't been cleaned in a month—"

Lili's jaw dropped. "How could it possibly be that dirty? Tony just cleaned it!"

Susan frowned. "How do you know that?"

"Because…because he told me, that's what he does on Saturdays, when the girls are gone. Cleans house. But children are messy! And Daphne just washed her hands."

Frowning slightly, Susan said gently, "Of course children are messy. But a clean house encourages them to be neater, don't you think?"

Lili thought of all the clean sinks and floors her brothers

had trashed immediately after she'd scrubbed them and almost laughed. Thought of the kitchen she'd spent all afternoon cleaning which had apparently either escaped the woman's notice or which obviously didn't meet Susan Pellegrino's impossible standards. "Not in my experience. And Tony's doing the best he can, he's wonderful with the girls and he loves them so much—"

Blushing, Lili faced the window again, her arms tightly crossed over her stomach.

"Lili? Is everything all right?"

Keep your mouth shut, this is none of your business, you don't know these people, Tony can take care of himself—

"I didn't mean to eavesdrop," she said as calmly as she could manage, "but…" She turned back. "You and your husband want the girls to come live with you?"

Her expression once more slipping into neutral, Susan walked over to the window, massaging lotion into her knuckles. "Lou and I have been discussing the possibility for a long time," she said softly. "I hadn't realized he'd bring the subject up tonight, though." Her gaze swung back to Lili. "What did Tony say?"

"What do you think he said? The very idea appalled him."

Susan sighed. "Not that I'm surprised. I'd just hoped…" She cleared her throat. "It's just…you people from the large families, you have no idea what it's like when you lose your only child. The crater it leaves in your hearts. Your lives." Tears glimmered in her eyes. "The girls are all we have left of Marissa. And we can offer them so much, take the burden off Tony, at least for a while—"

"The girls are all Tony has left, too! How could you even consider taking them away from him?"

"We're only thinking of what's best for them. And for Tony, too. He's obviously overwhelmed, even if he won't admit it—"

"Then help him—help the girls—right here!" Lili said,

startling herself. "Hire a housekeeping service or an au pair or something! And you already see the girls, what? Nearly every weekend? That's already a lot more than most grand-parents get!"

Susan calmly returned to her open bag, snapped shut the tube of lotion and dropped it back inside. "Clearly, Tony has a very staunch ally."

Realizing how close she'd come to showing her hand—a hand that wasn't even hers by rights to begin with—Lily strode back to the counter and the undressed salad. "Tony was…very sweet to me, the summer I was here," she said, dousing the pale greens with olive oil. The only lettuce she'd found in the vegetable bin was a head of old iceberg, the outer leaves wilted and rusty. But the inside was at least edible, if boring. "He didn't have to be, but he was. Especially since he was already going out with your daughter. I've never for-gotten his kindness, that's all."

"And now all these years later," Susan said, "you've got his back."

"Something like that, I suppose."

"You're blushing."

"It's warm in here."

After a long silence, Tony's mother-in-law said, very gently, "Lou and I weren't initially big fans of Tony and Marissa getting married. We felt they were too young, that Marissa was limiting her opportunities…" Shaking her head, she smiled slightly. "But our daughter is…*was* extraordi-narily stubborn. As is Tony. We finally realized he'd do anything to have her. Do anything *for* her. He's…" The corners of her mouth lifted. "An admirable young man. Very…honorable. Decent." She paused. "Lou and I think the world of him."

"They why do you want to take away his children?"

"We just want to help, Lili. That's all. But my point is…"

Susan came to stand beside Lili, her expression earnest. "He loved our daughter very, very much. And a love like that…well. I'm sure you're smart enough to put the pieces together."

Lili met the older woman's gaze. "That Tony's heart is still broken?" she said, deadpan, wondering what this woman would think if she knew the truth. "That he's no more ready to form another attachment than he is to fly? Of course."

"Oh, I think this goes beyond his being ready. Seeing what he went through, during Marissa's illness and…after…" She picked up the garlic salt, frowned at it, then put it down again. "Of course he might remarry—one day, when the children are ready to accept someone in Marissa's place—but I think it's safe to say he'll never love anyone again the way he loved our daughter. You might want to keep that in mind. And you might want to watch how much vinegar you're putting on that salad."

Lili slammed down the bottle. "Do you really think you're saying something I don't already know? That I can't see how much pain Tony's in? And Claire…" She lowered her eyes for a moment. "Even if I weren't returning to Hungary in a few weeks, I know all about trying to wedge yourself into a space when you know you'll never fit. I've had plenty of practice, believe me."

She dumped in a little more olive oil to counteract the vinegar. "But—forgive me for speaking out of turn—you've got no right deciding Tony's entire future, either. Or how or what he's supposed to feel. A man that good, that giving, deserves to be loved." *For the long haul, dammit,* Lili thought, madly mixing the greens as something fiery blossomed inside her. "He also deserves to be supported, not rescued. Because—"

"Burgers are ready," Tony said, popping in the back door, frowning when he clearly realized he'd interrupted their conversation. When he looked at Lili, she gave her head a small shake. Dear God—another dozen words and she'd have come this close to letting his secret slip.

"So's the salad," she said brightly, clamping her hands around the bowl to carry it outside, knowing full well the look Susan gave Tony behind her back.

Chapter Seven

A good half hour passed before Tony found a moment talk to Lili without anybody else in earshot. Burger in tow, he casually lowered his butt onto the chair opposite hers at the outside table, feeling like he should be passing off a briefcase of stolen dough. "What the hell happened in there?"

Lili sighed, her eyes fixed on Susan, pushing Josie in the baby swing. "I overheard Lou's suggesting they take the girls. I guess I came to your defense a little strongly."

Tony looked up from his burger. "You did that for me? And the girls?"

"Duh." She shoved a piece of anemic lettuce into her mouth, muttering, "How dare they?" around it.

Ed slinked past; Tony grabbed him to snag a crumpled napkin out of the his mouth. "Just a regular little she-wolf, aren'tcha?"

"Grrr," she said, and he smiled, thinking that her craziness—and by now, he had no doubt she was as crazy as the rest of the family—was like unexpected fireworks in a starless sky. Fleeting, yeah, but still nice.

"Like I said—I can handle Marissa's parents. Lou backed right down, if you noticed."

Lili's eyes touched his. "For how long?"

Tony bit into his burger. Set it back down on the plate. "They mean well. And this whole thing is killin' 'em, I know that. Doesn't mean they have a shot in hell of gettin' the girls." He gently bumped her knee with his. "But thanks for bein' on my side—"

"Lili!" Daphne called from the garden. "The radishes're coming up! Come see!"

"Guess I've been summoned." Her salad abandoned, she smiled slightly at Tony. "Just being a friend," she said, and the fireworks burst again, that brief moment of surprise, of sucked-in breath and amazement. "However, as soon as I've admired Daph's radishes, I think I'll take my leave. To stay longer would only cause more anxiety."

Tony tensed. "What makes you say that?"

"Um…Susan warned me off?"

"You're kidding."

Lili let out a dry laugh. "Not that it was necessary. I mean, I've just spent the better part of the last several years in isolation. Of my own choosing, yes. But I'd be a complete fool to walk right from that situation into one where…" Her mouth clamped shut.

"Where, what?"

She stood, glancing away for a moment before returning her gaze to his. "I told our aunt I missed being needed. But that's only half true. Because what *I* need, is to be *wanted*. For myself. And…I don't think that's happened, really. Ever. And despite what you say," she said, her words coming faster and faster, "I know when you look at me you're only seeing an older version of who I was fourteen years ago. You were angry and vulnerable then, and you're even angrier and more vulnerable now—"

"Li-*li!*"

"Coming, sweetie!" she called to Daphne, then turned back to Tony. "And that's perfectly okay, Tony, I swear. I'm glad to be your friend, to help however I can. But…" She took a deep breath. "Susan's warning was unnecessary."

Tony looked deep into Lili's eyes, gone a cloudy blue as the sun tilted west. "Any reason why you're telling me all this?"

"Yes," she said simply, then brushed past him and out into the yard, where she squatted by Daph with her arm around her waist, while Claire—and Marissa's mother—kept a watchful, wary eye on the whole proceeding.

Well. That just shot to hell the prospect of sleeping *that* night, didn't it?

You know, really, none of this has anything to do with you.
During the week or so since the cookout, Lili had probably reminded herself of this indisputable fact no less than a hundred times. As in, every time she thought of Tony. Which happened approximately every five minutes of every waking hour. Since clearly she was never going to sleep well again, that was a lot of thinking about Tony.

"Which will never do," she muttered to herself, smartly turning the page of the British chick lit novel she was translating for her Hungarian publisher, although she'd read the same page three times with no comprehension whatsoever. Might make translating it a trifle difficult.

They hadn't seen each other since then, there being no real reason to. Good thing, since Lili couldn't get the look in Tony's eyes when she left out of her mind. A soulful look, like an unclaimed dog at an animal shelter, resigned to its fate.

Doesn't matter what sort of signals he was sending out—
And even she knew there were signals, unintentional or no.

—the man's an emotional wreck.

She turned a page.

So you did the right thing, laying it on the line like that.

She shifted on her aunt's plastic-shrouded sofa, wincing when the backs of her thighs stuck.

And anyway, he was only using you as a sounding board—

The book sailed across the living room to bounce off the fireplace hearth. The obese retriever hauled himself to his feet to go investigate, only to collapse again with a groan. Groaning herself, Lili sank into the corner of the sofa, pouting like a teenager. Because she liked Tony. Liked being around him. Missed him when she wasn't. And all the logic in the world couldn't change any of that. She'd never really had to deal much with wanting things she couldn't have—not for years, at least—and doing so now was not sitting well.

Beside her, the landline rang. Without even checking the display, Lili plucked the phone off the end table.

"Lili?" said a slightly familiar voice. "It's Violet. Rudy's wife? We met at Magda's birthday party—" this came out nearly like "patty" "—a couple weeks ago?"

"Oh. Hi, Violet. Magda and Benny aren't here—"

"That's okay, it's actually you I wanna talk to, anyway."

"Me? Why?"

"Okay, I know this is last minute," the redhead said, "but we had a cancellation—an anniversary party, the family was supposedta take the whole inn—from Wednesday through Friday. I tried calling Tony, but his cell's not picking up and I'm just gettin' his machine on his home phone. But if you guys could make it then, that would be great."

Sure the cushions had muffled her hearing, Lili struggled to sit upright. "What do you mean, *you guys?*"

"Uh-oh…he didn't say anything, did he?"

"Um, no…"

"Honestly, men. Can't live with 'em, can't kill 'em." She

laughed. "You must've thought I was a few sandwiches short of picnic, goin' on and on when you had no clue what I was talking about. Anyway…when we were down there, we invited Tony and the girls up, said he should bring you, too. So consider this your official invitation—"

"Um…" Lili lunged for the first thought that scuttled across her brain. "That's very sweet of you, really…but I think Tony's got plans for the rest of the week. With the girls."

"Really? Rudy's mom seemed to think they were just rotting away in that big old house, not really doing much of anything. So what could it hurt to ask, right? Because God knows when we're gonna having another opening like this for the rest of the summah. He's never been up here, and you must be goin' batty by now at Magda's. Don't get me wrong, I love her to death, but Mag's like one of her rich desserts, she's better in small doses. Right?"

Lili waited for the dust to settle, then chuckled. "That's very true." Then she had a thought. "I suppose I could come up on my own?"

"If it doesn't work out with Tony, sure, why not? Hey, you like to shop? We've got an outlet mall up heah that'll knock your socks off…"

After a few more minutes devoted to the wonders of southern New Hampshire, Violet rang off. The buzzing in Lili's ears had barely stopped, however, when the phone rang again. Seeing Tony's name on the display, she flinched as though pricked by a thorn. Letting the answering machine pick up was certainly tempting. As well as cowardly and childish. Besides, she supposed she should at least *tell* him about the invitation.

"Oh, good—it's you." Was it bad that his voice sent actual shivers up her spine? Was it worse that Peter's voice had never tingled a single vertebra? "I need to ask a favor."

"Why are you whispering?"

"Because apparently I'm raising bats," he whispered. "Do you think you could come over and watch the older girls tomorrow morning while I take…" his voice softened even more "…JoJo to get the test done? I hate to ask, but you're the only one who knows, if I ask anybody in the family they'll be all over me with a hundred questions—"

"I'd be glad to," Lili said, because what else was she going to say? "What are you going to tell the girls?"

"That I'm taking the baby in for a check-up. I figure—"

The next part of whatever he was said was muffled as he apparently put his hand over the phone. A few seconds later, he was back.

"Sorry about that. Anyway. The kids aren't exactly big fans of the doctor's office, so nobody's gonna wanna tag along."

"Er…Claire's not exactly a big fan of me, either."

"For an hour, she can deal. I mean, unless you're uncomfortable…?" This said with a slight begging edge to his voice.

"I suppose I can deal for an hour, too. What time do you want me there?"

"Nine?"

"Nine it is. Oh! I almost forgot! Violet just called, something about our going up to their inn?"

"Crap, I didn't think they were actually serious."

"Apparently, since you never mentioned it. But the invitation's for Wednesday through Friday. I told them you were busy, but Violet didn't shake off that easily."

Tony almost chuckled. "No. She wouldn't." Then he sobered. "You told 'em I was busy?"

Lili couldn't quite read his tone. "I thought…I didn't think…yes," she finally said. "Because we couldn't possibly go up there together. For obvious reasons."

A second passed before Tony said, "From everything I've heard, it's a really great place."

"I'm sure it is, but—"

"And hey—free vacation."

Lily sat up a little straighter on the sofa. "You can't possibly think this would be a good idea?"

"Oh, I think it's a terrible idea," he said, not a hint of humor in his voice. She heard his screen door bang open, a car going by, the drone of a cicada. "You and me, together—"

"With the kids, of course," she said, her stomach going all jittery.

"Somehow, I don't think having the kids around would make much difference one way or the other, but that's just me."

She stilled. "What are you saying?"

"What the hell do you think I'm saying?"

"You're…attracted to me?"

"*Duh,*" he said, and she pressed her hand to her mouth. "God knows, I don't wanna be, I can't act on it, I can't think of anything worse for either of us—"

Earth to Lili.

"—but yeah. I am. And if I wasn't so braindead I probably wouldn't've said anything. But I'm tired…" She heard him push out a sigh. "I'm tired of secrets, Lili. Tired of pretending." For some reason, she visualized him leaning one hand against a support post, the phone clamped to his ear. Saw him so clearly, in fact, her hand lifted, as though to touch him. *Silly girl.*

Now she pushed out a sigh littered with a thousand shards of unfulfilled dreams.

"But I'm also tired of us bein' cooped up in this damn house, this damn *town,*" Tony said. "So I'm thinking, maybe a couple days away wouldn't be such a bad idea. Maybe it would maybe help Claire shake that freakin' cloud that follows her everywhere." He paused. "Maybe it would give me something to do beside sit here and worry about…the results."

Oh, she thought. "How long does it take?"

"Forty-eight hours."

Her heart twisted, knowing it would be the longest two days of his life. "So take the kids, why do I have to go?"

"Because you've never been to New Hampshire," he finally said, then hung up.

"Why can't *I* watch Daphne while you're gone?" Claire said the next morning, shadowing Tony from room to room as he looked for Josie's other sandal. Which, natch, had gone missing in the middle of the night even though he distinctly remembered putting them both on top of her toy chest before her bath.

"Because you're ten and it's against the law," Tony muttered, thinking, *Oh, hell,* when he spotted the damn shoe next to the dog's water dish. Josie clinging to his hip, he squatted to pick up the sandal, breathing out a profound sigh of relief that, except for a couple of canine tooth dents in the rubber, it was otherwise intact. He plunked down on a kitchen chair to insert foot in sandal. "And there's way too many cops in this family to take that chance."

"But why is *Lili* watching us?"

"Because everybody else was busy," Tony said, wondering how many lies, white or otherwise, the average parent dispensed over the course of eighteen years. Or longer. "And what've you got against Lili, anyway? She's a nice lady."

Claire gave him one of those if-I-have-to-explain-what's-the-point? looks. The same one he'd seen way too many times from her mother. Once upon a time, he'd found it endearing. "That's probably her now," he said when both the doorbell and the dog sounded. "Go let her in."

"Daphne can do it."

"See?" Tony said, getting to his feet. "Exactly why you can't watch her on your own, you'd let her open the door to anybody."

Claire's mouth fell open. "Ohmigod! Of course I wouldn't do that! You just *said* it was Lili! God—"

"Well," Lili said brightly from the kitchen doorway, Daphne at her side and more grocery bags dangling from her hands. Amused eyes bounced off Tony's before settling on Claire. "What did he do this time?" she said, and the girl's gaze flew to hers.

"He…" Her cheeks flamed. "Nothing."

"Really?" She looked at Tony again. "Because I could have sworn I heard you teasing the poor child."

"Naw, I was just—"

"My father," Lili said to Claire, "would tease me to distraction. Of course, eventually I realized that was his *strange*—" another glance at Tony "—way of showing his love. But when I was your age? Torture, I tell you. Pure torture."

Wow, point to you, Tony thought as Claire regarded Lili in stunned silence for several seconds before curiosity apparently got the better of her. "What's in the bags?"

Lili grinned. "I thought we could make plum dumplings," she said, blue eyes sparkling behind her glasses.

And behind Claire's glasses, The Look of Utter Horror. "You mean, with actual *plums* in them?"

"Well…yes. It's, um, a traditional Hungarian dish, I used to love them when I was a child—"

"I don't *think* so," Claire said, storming out of the kitchen. She was halfway up the stairs before Tony caught up with her.

"Claire. Come back here. *Now.*"

She turned, miserable. "You know I hate plums, Dad, they make me gag—"

"I understand that. But Lili didn't do anything to warrant that reaction. So you march yourself back down and apologize—"

"Tony," Lili said behind him. "That's not necessary, really—"

"Yeah. It is. Claire?"

Her arms tightly folded over her chest, she glowered at the riser below her for a moment, then came down the stairs far enough to see Lili. "I'm sorry," she mumbled, then lifted her eyes. "But I really *don't* like plums. Would it be okay…" She shoved her hair behind her ear. "Would you mind if I stayed in my room and read instead?"

Lili glanced at Tony, who nodded, before saying to Claire, "Of course not. You go right ahead." Then she turned to Daphne, who was tugging her skirt. Leave it to that one to have a front row seat. Kid lived for this stuff.

"I'll help you make them." She was also a world-class brownnoser.

"Oh. Good. Thank you. Why don't you go unload all the bags onto the kitchen table, then, and I'll be right in?"

His middle child skipped off, humming happily, as his oldest tromped upstairs. A moment later they heard her door click shut. "Sorry about that," Tony muttered, grabbing both baby and car keys. He turned to Lili, who, as usual, seemed remarkably unfazed by it all. "Civilizing kids is a lot harder than it looks."

She smiled. "She'll be fine. *We'll* be fine."

He wanted to kiss her so badly he thought the top of his head would come off. "Well," he said, lowering his eyes to the baby. "Guess I can't put this off any longer."

Tony was nearly out to the car before he realized Lili had followed them to stand in the driveway with her arms crossed, a breeze fluttering her flippy little skirt around her knees. "I take it you haven't mentioned the New Hampshire trip?" she said as he belted Josie into her car seat. He straightened; she'd messily twisted her hair up with a couple sticks poking through it, so half of it was floating around her face. In the sunlight, it had a lot more gold in it than he would've thought.

"No. Not yet. When I get back's soon enough. That way

they have less than twenty-four hours to drive me nuts about it." He propped one hand on the car's roof, still cool in the early morning shade. "I thought you didn't wanna go."

Strands of hair teased her cheeks for a moment before she said, "Actually, I do. Very much. Whether I should or not, though…" She glanced up at the upstairs window.

"Her room's in back, she can't hear us. But it's okay, you don't hafta spell it out."

"I just don't want to add to anyone's distress." Her cheeks flushed. "I'm only here for the summer, Tony. And heaven only knows when I'll be back. If I'll be back."

"Because you're gonna go off and find your life and all that."

"Right," she said, the corners of her mouth lifting. "So the logical side of my brain thinks I should probably keep my distance." Her gaze speared his. "For many reasons."

"And what does the illogical side of your brain think?"

"That logic is hugely overrated. That—" her blush deepened, making her eyes even bluer "—that I don't exactly have a lot to show for nearly thirty years of doing the 'right' thing, do I?"

Tony slammed shut the car's back door and yanked his open, knowing his frustration had virtually nothing to do with her and everything to do with feeling like he was the butt of some sick joke. Finally he looked back at Lili, knowing damn well what he should do and not having the least interest in doing it, for probably much the same reasons as her.

"Why don't you see how it goes with the girls today?" he said mildly. "Then let me know tonight what you decide."

"Fair enough," she said, turning back to the house. This time, though, it wasn't her backside he was fixated on, but her hair, flashing gold in the morning sun. He could practically feel it, slippery and warm between his fingers, against his mouth…

"I am so screwed," he muttered, climbing behind the wheel and jerking the gear shift into Reverse.

* * *

"Over there, Ed!" Daphne yelled at the dog, who'd been doing acrobatics for the past ten minutes trying to catch a fly and keeping both Lili and her sous-chef in stitches. The dog spun around, snapping several times at the buzzing insect until, frustrated, he started barking at it.

"Yeah, that'll show it," Lili said, and Daphne dissolved into at least her tenth giggle fit of the morning.

"Look, Lili! He got it!"

"Are you sure?"

"Uh-huh—he's chewing!"

"Ewwww," they said at the same time, then cracked up all over again—

"What on earth is going on in here?" Claire said from the doorway, clearly annoyed at being left out of the fun.

"Ed caught a fly!" Daphne said from stool next to the counter where she'd been smushing together confectioner's sugar and cinnamon with a fork. "An' then he ate it! Hey, Claire—you should come help—we're making plum dumplings!"

"I'd rather eat the fly," Claire grumbled, sidling over to the fridge and trying not to show interest in the proceedings. "Sheesh, it was so noisy down here I couldn't read."

"Sorry," Lili mumbled, exchanging a look with Daphne, who giggled again. And then brushed her forehead with the back of her hand. Sugar everywhere.

"Come on, Claire," the little girl said, dimpling at Lili. "It's fun."

"Claire doesn't like plums," Lili said mildly, cutting the already made potato dough into squares. "Actually, neither do I, unless they're in dumplings."

The ten-year-old edged closer, eyeing their workstation. "That's…weird."

"Isn't it? We're ready to wrap the dough around the fruit. Wanna try?"

"It looks messy."

"Oh, it is," Lili said as Daphne trooped from counter to table with the bowl of cinnamon sugar in her hands. And splotches of flour on her face and bits of potato in her hair. At Claire's gasp, Lili bit her lip to keep from laughing.

"Ohmigod, Daph! What happened to you?"

"Daph helped make the dough," Lili said, and Claire looked at her as if she'd just announced they'd invited Martians to lunch.

"Nana's picking us up in an hour to take us shopping! In the *Cadillac!*" Tears bulged in her eyes. "She'll have an absolute fit when she sees Daphne!"

This was news to Lili. "Oh?" she said, pinning the child with her gaze. "Funny, your father didn't mention it."

"That's because…he d-didn't know. Nana just c-called and said she was on her way."

Lili could call the child on the lie, since the phone hadn't rung. And for a moment she had to fight the blow to her own ego that Claire would go to such elaborate lengths to get away from her. Then she remembered what it had felt like to be a ten-year-old who basically hated her life.

"Well, not to worry…Daph's washable." Then, out of nowhere, she heard herself add, "Nobody expects you to be responsible for your sister, Claire." She paused. "Or anybody else."

"That's what I keep *trying* to tell her," Daphne put in, waving her hands. "That she's not in charge of me and JoJo. But will she listen?" The younger girl blew out a sigh. "No."

Tamping down another laugh, Lili got up to gently lead a sniffling Claire to the sink, where she dampened a paper towel. "Put this on your eyes, it will keep them from getting puffy."

Removing her glasses to press the compress to one eye, the girl peered at Lili with the other, glimmering with cautious trust. "Mom used to do this, too. With the towel."

"It's a girl thing," Lili said. "So. We have an hour?"

"Yeah, about."

"That's plenty of time to finish and for Daphne to have her shower. And if you don't wish to help—"

"No, it's okay." She shrugged. "It's not like I've got anything else to do." The towel abandoned, Claire frowned at the squares of dough already laid out on the floured table. "So what's next?"

Her heart fluttering at the small step toward détente, Lili showed Claire how to wrap the dough around chunks of sweet-tart plum, pinching the edges closed to form little balls before lowering them into the big pot of boiling water on the stove. Both girls—and Ed—stood in rapt attention beside her, although the dog couldn't see inside the bubbling pot.

"How do you know when they're done?" Claire asked.

"When they pop up. Like that!" Lili said, smiling, as one by one the dumplings bobbed to the surface of the bubbling water, which she carefully removed with a slotted spoon. "Now we roll them the breadcrumbs," she said, transferring the platter of hot, cooked dumplings to the table to be gently coated in fragrant, buttery breadcrumbs.

"And now the sugar?" Daphne asked.

"And now the sugar."

Lili stood aside, quietly coaching the girls as they sprinkled the warm, crunchy dumplings with the sugar mixture, the fragrance of cinnamon and warm fruit and butter filling the old kitchen, filling Lili's head with silly notions she dared not indulge for long. The dumplings all frosted and sparkly under the fake Tiffany lamp suspended over the table, Claire looked at her—without a frown—and Lily nearly groaned with yearning for a home and family of her own.

"Can we eat one?"

"Not yet. Better give them a few minutes for the fruit to cool. I don't want you to burn your mouths."

"And you," Claire said to Daphne, "go take your bath. Hair, too."

Lili frowned at the younger girl. "Can you do that alone?"

"Of course," Daphne said as she slid off her chair. "I'm not a baby, sheesh." Then she pointed at them. "But no eating the dumplings until I get back!"

Then she trounced off, potato-flecked curls fluttering indignantly. A moment later, Claire got up, too, looking unsure of what came next.

"It's okay," Lili said, "you can go."

"Don't you need some help cleaning up?"

"That's all ri—" *Oh, for heaven's sake—are you insane?* "I'd love some help. Although it seems Ed's already taken care of the floor," she said, watching the dog frantically sucking up every crumb he could find.

The giggle was short, and barely audible, but it was definitely a giggle.

They worked in virtual silence for several minutes, Lili hardly daring to breathe for fear she'd break the spell. Finally, though, she heard a soft, "It must've been so cool, growing up in the circus."

"Oh. Well…not so much, actually."

She could feel the girl's frown. "How come?"

"Traveling all the time sucks, if you don't like it. And it's deadly dull if you're not performing."

"You didn't?"

"Oh, dear God, no. My father used to say I was the most uncoordinated child in Hungary."

"That's awful."

She laughed. "But true. All I wanted, when I was your age, was to be normal. To go to a normal school and do normal things." She let out a dramatic sigh. "To have parents who didn't wear tights and sequins, who didn't *fly*, for goodness sake!"

A second giggle made Lili's heart jump. "Yeah, I could see how that would be a little strange."

"For the other circus kids, that *was* normal. And they loved it. For me…no. It didn't help, either, that I had the self-esteem of a slug." Claire frowned. "I didn't like myself very much."

There went that curious look again. "Why?"

"Because…I was all pointy angles. And clumsy. And my nose was too big and my mouth too wide, and I hated these—" she pointed to her protruding incisors "—because my brothers called me Vampira all the time. And," she continued as Claire giggled *again,* "I never felt I had anything in common with the other kids my age. Sometimes, I was tempted to wonder if I really *was* a vampire kid my parents had gotten from the gypsies or something."

"I know how that goes," Claire said with a solemn nod. "Not about the vampire thing, but the rest of it? Yeah." She looked at the dumplings. Taking her cue, Lili leaned over and touched one.

"I think they're ready."

"Oh. Um…shouldn't we wait for Daphne?"

"She'll never know." Lili held out the plate to her. "Unless you tell."

The child reached for one, then pulled back, frowning. "But I hate plums."

"Do you really hate them? Or just think you do?" When Claire's eyes shot to Lili's, she shrugged, even as she suddenly felt so strongly for the little girl she ached. *I know how hard it is,* she wanted to say, *forcing yourself to try new things. To move past "safe."* "One bite. If you don't like it, I promise my feelings won't be hurt."

Claire hesitated, then gingerly—as though the dumpling might explode—plucked one off the pile. After a few seconds' intense contemplation, she jerked her hair behind one ear and took the tiniest bite possible…only to shudder when the tart fruit juices hit her tongue. Lili held her breath, fully expecting the girl to spit it out. Instead, she not only swallowed, but took a second bite. Without shuddering, this time.

"So…what's the verdict?"

A shrug preceded the rest of the dumpling vanishing into her mouth. "S'okay," she said, chewing. "Once you get used to it." *One could say that about most things in life,* Lili thought as the child asked, "May I have another one?"

"Go for it."

Claire wriggled into a kitchen chair, to better savor her treat, apparently. In the midst of catching a dribble of plum juice on her chin, however, she said, "Are you just being nice to me because of Dad?"

So much for détente. "I could ask the same of you, you know."

The girl's eyes flashed to hers. Then she shrugged, a small, sad what's-the-point? gesture that completely cancelled out the spoken, "Whatever," that followed it.

Sighing, Lili dropped into another chair to meet the girl's eyes. "Claire, I know there's…stuff between you and me, even if I'm not completely sure what that stuff is. But for a few minutes, I thought we'd moved beyond that. At least I had." Far too perceptive by half, the child watched her, waiting. Lili sat back in the chair, her arms folded over her chest. "I'm not going to pretend I know exactly how you're feeling—that would be beyond stupid—but sometimes, when you get certain expressions on your face? They remind a lot of the expressions I used to see in my own mirror. So I feel, just a little, as if I've known you for a long time. And that's a good thing."

Claire took another bite, her brows knit as she turned the remaining chunk of dumpling over and over in her fingers. "So Dad has nothing to do with it?"

"Well, obviously I wouldn't even be here if it weren't for him. But he's not why I'm being nice to you. I'm being nice to you because…you're a very interesting person."

"Me?" Claire said, pressing plumy fingers to her white top. Oops.

"Yes, you. You've brave, you're not afraid to speak your mind, which a lot of women—" Lili raised her hand "—have problems with. And you clearly love your sisters and father very, very much."

"You think I'm brave?"

Lili smiled. "You ate the dumpling, didn't you?"

Still frowning, Claire licked her fingers, then looked straight at Lili. "If I ask you something, will you tell me the truth?"

"I'll certainly try."

"Do you like Dad or not? And I don't mean as a—" she made quote marks in the air "—friend."

Lili leaned over, picking a dumpling off the pile and biting into it. *Perfect,* she thought as juice dripped down her chin. Claire handed her a napkin. "Yes," she said, wiping her mouth. "I do."

Claire's eyes never left hers. "Does he like you?"

"You'd have to ask him that, I can't answer for him." She took another bite, wiped her mouth again. "But I can say that, sometimes, with grownups…liking each other doesn't mean…" She searched for the right words. "Doesn't mean serious, or forever, or…anything, really. Sometimes, the timing's all wrong, or there are other things, or people, you have to think about." Finishing off the dumpling, she shrugged. "It's complicated."

The child let out a long sigh. "Yeah. Tell me about it."

Lili smiled, even though her stomach felt as if she'd eaten the entire plate of dumplings on her own. "Even if…things were different, I think it's pretty safe to say your father would never do anything to upset you. Or push you into something you're not ready for." Lili paused. "And neither would I."

The girl's eyes lifted again. "You promise?"

"Cross my heart," Lili said, doing just that, then said, "You see, the timing isn't good for me, either."

"You mean…like you don't want a boyfriend right now?"

Lili's mouth twitched, even as she realized she was having trouble with that logic thing again. That her pull toward Tony was in direct opposition to an almost desperate need to figure out who she was and what her place in the grand scheme of things was supposed to be. "You're an incredibly smart little girl, aren't you?" she said, and Claire lowered her eyes, blushing. Then she added, "If something's right, it has to be right for everybody. Does that make sense?"

Claire reached for another dumpling before finally nodding. "Yeah, I guess," she said, just as a dripping, towel-clad Daphne appeared in the doorway. "No fair! You said you wouldn't start without me!"

Her hair a mass of sopping corkscrews, she tromped across the tile floor, leaving behind a trail of wet footprints, to snatch one of the dumplings off the pile and shove the whole thing into her mouth. A moment later she ran to the trash can to spit it out, then to the sink for a glass of water which she gulped down as if her mouth was on fire. "Grossioso!" she said once she came up for air. "And you people actually *ate* those things?"

Claire and Lili looked at each other and burst out laughing…a moment before the doorbell rang.

"I'll get it," Daphne said, letting out a shriek when Claire nearly tackled her to the floor.

"You can't answer the door, you're naked!"

"Am not, I'm wearing a towel!" Daphne yelled after Claire as the older girl stormed out…only to return a few seconds later with a puzzled look on her face.

"I looked through the peephole, just to make sure it was

Nana? But it's not, it's some guy I've never seen before. So I didn't open the door."

"Good girl. Was he holding a clipboard? Pamphlets?" Lili'd already gotten the lowdown from Magda, who you opened the door to and who you didn't.

"Did he look like a weirdo?" Daphne put in.

"He looks *fine,*" Claire huffed. "I just don't know him."

"Ed, come," Lili said, beckoning the lean, mean, fly-eating machine to follow her and the girls down the hall. Grasping the dog's collar, she opened the door.

"Maybe I help you?" she asked the square-jawed man on the other side, blond and crisp and creased, the type of man whose life was probably governed by some bit of technology smaller than a deck of cards.

Then he said, "This *is* Tony Vaccaro's house, isn't it?" and Lili got a very strong feeling that life had just come crashing down around his perfectly coiffed head.

Chapter Eight

Within like a second of Lili's opening the door, Claire got one of her bad feelings. She even felt the back of her neck prickle, like when she was little and had to go pee in the middle of the night, and the house was all dark and spooky.

Without thinking, she took Daphne's hand and inched closer to Lili. The stranger didn't look at either of them. With his sunglasses on, Claire couldn't decide if he was angry or sad or both, but whatever it was, his face creeped her out.

"Tony's not available at the moment," Lili said, fighting to keep Ed, who on his hind legs was nearly as tall as Lili, from jumping up on the man. Only to lick him, but the guy didn't know that. "Who shall I say was here—?"

"Will he be back soon?"

"If you leave a number, I could have him call you."

Claire noticed Lili didn't invite him inside to wait. Also, that she blocked both Claire and Daph with her body. But instead of answering, the man turned and went back down the steps and out to his car, a small, fancy one with no top, like Gramps drove.

"Who was it?" Daph asked after he drove away.

"I have no idea." Lili let Ed go, then closed the door, looking from Claire to Daph. "Neither of you recognized him?"

"Uh-uh," they both said. Claire noticed Lili's hands were shaking, a little. Then she smiled and told them to go get dressed, they didn't want to keep their grandmother waiting. Except before she'd finished her sentence, practically, the door opened—everybody jumped, including the dog—but it was only Daddy and JoJo. Daddy gave Lili a really weird look, and she gave him one right back.

Which only made Claire's neck prickle even harder as she and Daph went upstairs.

Tony waited until he was sure the girls were in their rooms before spinning on a very pale Lili. "What happened?" he whispered, setting Josie down. "You look like you just saw a ghost."

"No, no ghost," she said, palming her cheek before lifting her eyes to Tony's. "A real live man. Here, asking for you. Well-dressed, light hair. Couldn't tell his eye color, he was wearing sunglasses. But he drives an expensive looking sports car. A Jaguar, perhaps. Silver."

His mind racing, Tony crossed the entryway on autopilot to wrest one of the dog's toys out of Josie's hands, barely hearing the baby's howl of protest. "Don't know the car. But…" After another glance upstairs, he turned back to Lili. "Who else could it be?"

Shaking her head, Lili sat on the boot-and-scarf bench by the front door, smiling when Josie made a beeline for her and crawled up into her lap. A second later she'd snuggled against Lili's chest with her thumb in her mouth; Lili gently palmed the baby's head, stroking her fine hair. "Why does this feel so good?" she asked, shifting slightly to settle Josie more securely on her lap.

Even over the sudden surge of acid in his gut, Tony's mouth twitched. "So you don't sell 'em to the highest bidder when they hit puberty?"

Lili chuckled, resting her cheek on top of the Josie's head as she looked up, her eyes soft with sympathy. "When will you know? About the test?"

The bench creaked when Tony lowered his carcass beside her. Josie immediately decided she wanted him again. "Sometime Thursday," he said, strongly tempted to put the kid in the car and strike out for parts unknown.

A quick, light squeeze of his wrist preceded, "If it's still okay, I would like to go to New Hampshire with you and the girls."

He twisted to look at her profile. "You sure?"

"I think Claire and I came to an understanding," she said over the sound of little feet clattering down the stairs. "I even got her to giggle."

"You're puttin' me on."

"Not a bit of it. More than once, even." As Tony shook his head, amazed, Lili added, "Although if she still has a problem with my tagging along, I won't go—"

The girls hit the bottom of the stairs at the same time the doorbell rang, giving Tony only a second to frown at their strangely spiffy outfits before Daph rushed to the picture window in the living room and announced, "Okay, this time it really is Nana!"

"And why is that?" he asked his red-faced—and usually glib—oldest daughter. But before she could answer, his mother-in-law swept through the door, all tanned and toned in a neat little tennis dress and sparkling white shoes to match.

"No, Ed, get *down!* DOWN! Honestly, Tony, you really must get that dog in obedience school—hello, darlings!"

Susan said, dispensing hugs and kisses like she hadn't just seen the kids the day before…a flurry of activity that came to a screeching halt the instant she laid eyes on Lili.

"Oh," she said, obviously confused. "Lili. How nice to see you again—"

"Dad had to take JoJo to the doctor," Daph said before Tony could muzzle her, "so Lili stayed with us. We made plum dumplings, but they're seriously gross—"

"They were not," Claire put in.

"Were, too—"

"What do you mean," Susan said, "you took the baby to the doctor?"

"You ate plum dumplings?" Tony asked, flummoxed.

"Yeah," Claire said with a little smile at Lili. "They were actually pretty good—"

"Are you all right, sweetie?" Susan asked, palming JoJo's forehead.

"She's fine," Tony said. "Just a check-up."

"Oh. Well, then." Susan gave him a funny look, then smiled for her granddaughters. "Are you two ready to go?"

Tony looked at Claire again. "Go where?"

"Their grandmother invited them to go shopping for school," Lili said. "Sort of a last-minute thing, I gathered."

And yeah, he caught the slightly puzzled looks on both Claire's and Susan's faces. God save him from female conspiracies. "But school's not for weeks yet."

"Then now's the best time to shop," Susan said, taking Daphne's hand, "before the stores get crowded." Then she smiled at Tony, and he remembered Marissa talking about her and her mother's shopping expeditions, all-day affairs that often included pedicures and lunches at fancy restaurants…a tradition they'd kept up until nearly the end. He hated shopping, himself, but he could tell how much this meant to Susan, being able to do with her granddaughters what she could no longer do with her own daughter. "And besides," she said, looking genuinely happy for the first time in months, "tell me I'm not saving you hours of agony."

Tony chuckled. "Okay, you got me there. But they wear uniforms, so don't buy 'em a lot of stuff they can't wear. And they gotta be home by five, 'cause we're goin' on a trip tomorrow and I wanna get an early start."

At that, all eyes veered to him.

"What kind of trip, Tony—?"

"Really? Yay! Where are we going—?"

"What if I don't wanna go?"

"It's just for a cuppla days," he said to the group at large, "up to visit Rudy and Violet in New Hampshire. I didn't know about it myself until yesterday." He paused, not really wanting to do this in front of Susan, but better now than to a couple of cranky, malled-out kids. Then, because Susan would only find out later, anyway, he added, "And I've invited Lili to go along."

Daphne squealed another "Yay!" and wrapped her arms around Lili's hips, Claire went into dour mode and Susan looked like she'd just been goosed. Lili, however, bent over to look into Claire's eyes.

"But only if it's okay with you," she said softly.

Claire frowned. "Really?"

"Really—"

"Please say yes, Claire," Daphne said, clinging to Lili. A move obviously not sitting well with Susan. "Please?"

After a moment, Claire sighed. "Sure, why not?" she said, and Lili smiled, and all manner of untoward thoughts rose up in Tony's brain, despite his mother-in-law's pointed glance in his direction before she opened the front door.

"Girls, why don't you go on out to the car? Tony? We should, um, probably discuss what the girls need for school. Would you mind coming out with me for a moment?"

Leaving Josie behind with Lili—and trying to ignore Lili's raised brows—Tony followed Marissa's mother. "Don't start, Susan," he said in a low voice as soon as they got out on the porch and the girls were safely in the car. "I know what you're thinking—"

"What? What am I thinking? Besides the fact that you're rushing into another relationship when Marissa hasn't even been gone a year yet?"

Tony's face heated. "I'm not rushing into *anything*. Rudy and Violet invited us up to their inn on the spur of the moment and asked me if I'd like to bring her along, so that's what I'm doing. And that's *all* I'm doing."

"And did you see how attached Daphne already is? Did you?"

"Daphne attaches herself to everybody she meets, she's always been that way—"

"And what happens when Lili leaves?"

"She'll get over it."

"And will Claire?"

"What are you talkin' about? Claire's barely warming up to the woman—"

"And when she does," Susan said, genuine worry in her eyes, "she's going to fall hard. Harder than she's ready to deal with this soon after losing her mother. Tony…" She laid a hand on his arm. "I know how horribly lonely you must be. But for the children's sake, for *your* sake, please don't do anything you'll regret later—"

"Not about to. After everything I've been through these past months…" His throat working overtime, Tony looked away from the still-fresh pain in his mother-in-law's eyes. "Lili's a friend," he said at last. Which was true, his increasingly frequent more-than-friendly thoughts about her notwithstanding. "And if she can help Claire act and sound like a little girl again, instead of a crotchety old woman, I'm not gonna stop her."

"*We* can help her do that!"

"No, you can't. Because every time she looks at you, she sees her mother. Worse, she sees how much pain *you're* still in. And that's not to put down how much you and Lou have helped us, or how much you love the girls or they love you. Not at all. But I saw something in Claire's face today that I haven't seen in a long, long time, something good, and it just seems stupid not to run with that, you know?"

"It's just…" Susan's mouth thinned. "We don't want *you* to get hurt again, either," she said, then popped on her sunglasses, took a deep breath, and headed toward the Caddy, her tennis shoes barely making a sound on Tony's shady, root-cracked walk.

Lili scooted away from the window, crouching in front of Josie—who'd dragged her toy basket from the living room into the vestibule—just as Tony came back in. The door shut behind him, he leaned against it, one hand still on the knob. "So how much of that did you hear?"

She flushed. "What makes you think—?"

"Lili. Please."

"I got the important bits," she said on a rush of air, wrestling a stuffed cat out of Ed's mouth and handing it back to Josie, who sternly wagged her finger at the dog and said, "No, no, Ed—mine!" Lili smiled. "That she's worried about the girls becoming too attached to me." Her eyes met his. "That you're definitely not looking for…entanglements right now. Which we'd already established."

Tony pushed off the door, shoving his fingers into the front pockets of his jeans as he watched the baby. "Looking, not looking…either one takes more energy than I've got." Then he dropped back onto the bench, tightly gripping the edge on either side of his thighs. "But I had to say something to get Susan off my case. Off yours, too—"

"Yuck," Josie said, making a face before conking poor Ed on the head with the toy. "Kitty all wet. Bad Ed. Bad doggie."

At Ed's *What did I do?* look, Lili chuckled. Josie handed the soggy kitty to her; pensively wiping it on her skirt, Lili said, "You're giving me far too much credit about Claire, though."

"She *giggled,* Lil. Do you have any idea…?" He cleared his throat, then sagged against the bench's wooden back, pressing his thumb and forefinger into his eyes before saying, "Did the guy say he'd come back today?"

"He didn't say much of anything, really. Do you…do you want me to stay?"

"No, you go on," he said, smiling for Josie when she pranced back to him and crawled into his lap. "Wouldn't be anything you could do if he shows up again, anyway—"

"*My* daddy," Josie said, patting Tony's muscled forearm before threading her silky little arms around his neck. "Kiss kiss?"

"You got it, cutie," Tony said, bouncing a kiss off her puckered lips, looking at Lili over the baby's shoulder when she hugged her daddy again.

And the love and fear and longing in those deep brown eyes nearly did her in.

The early morning sun beating down on him at the end of the driveway, Tony checked his watch for what must've been the tenth time in as many minutes. Over in the yard, Daph and Josie and the Ed—who was going, too, Rudy had said their own dog, Simon, would get a kick out of it—were running around in circles and making enough noise to set off car alarms in Alaska.

"Maybe she changed her mind," Claire said, leaning over the open tailgate to shove in her backpack and not trying all that hard to hide her disappointment. Tony inwardly swore, thinking Susan was right, it *was* dumb, letting the girl get close to somebody who wasn't hanging around.

Maybe even dumber than letting *himself* get close to somebody who wasn't hanging around.

"Nah," he said, shooting Claire a smile before staring down the street, like he could will Lili to materialize. "I'm sure something must've just held her up."

"Did you call her?"

"Several times. Yes, both her cell and Magda's landline. Nobody answered…wait. Is that her? That's her, right? See, what did I tell you, that she'd be here, right?"

Claire frowned. Okay, that might've been overkill.

A minute later, his Uncle Benny pulled his verging-on-vintage Pontiac up behind the Volvo, leaning out of the window to yell, "Sorry we're late, this one—" he aimed a thumb in Lili's direction, a blur of arms and bags as she scrambled out of the passenger seat "—had to make a last-minute stop at the Rite Aid, and I got a flat, can you believe it? Haven't had one of those in probably twenty years—"

"And I forgot to charge my cell," Lili said, hot-footing it to the tailgate with a purse large enough to stash Ed in hanging from her shoulder as she dragged a small rolling case behind her. "And of course nobody was home to tell you what was going on…" Tony came up beside her to heft the case into the car, and she was very close and very warm, her scent rising up off her in brain-melting waves, and when he looked down into those oh-God-I'm-so-sorry eyes behind her glasses…

Uh, boy.

"S'okay," he said, one brand of anxiety sloughing off only to be replaced by something far scarier the instant she smiled. Fortunately, one of them had the presence of mind to break the eye contact—not Tony, however—after which they both thanked Benny for bringing her. Waving, his uncle backed out of the driveway and drove off.

The next five minutes was spent making sure the car was packed and the girls were emptied, that somebody had remembered to bring the dog's food and dish and diapers for the baby, whose potty skills were sketchy at best, and suddenly Tony heard Daphne say, "Isn't that the man who was here yesterday?" and he snapped his head around so hard his neck cracked.

Then he glanced at Lili, who nodded. And frowned. "Should we go inside?"

"Not necessary," Tony said mildly, offering a clearly troubled Claire a quick smile before he walked out to the street and down the half block to where the silver Jag was parked. At his approach, the man removed his sunglasses and got out, not looking a whole lot better than Tony felt. Wasn't until he got right up to the guy, however, that his stomach sank to his knees.

"Holy crap. Cole *Jamison?*"

The dude shot a quick look around, like Tony shouldn't've said his name out loud. Then his gaze veered to Tony's driveway. To Josie, safe in Lili's arms.

"You first," Tony said in a low voice.

"You're leaving?"

"For a couple of days. Don't worry, I'm not skippin' town. Well?"

Cole almost didn't seem to hear him, staring instead past Tony's shoulder, while Tony tried to absorb the irony. Two high school jocks, one from a blue-collar Italian family, the other from the same country-club set as Rissa's maternal grandparents, both with a thing for the same girl. How smug Tony'd felt, when he'd "won."

Cole's hand trembled when he rubbed his mouth. "She looks like me."

"She looks like Marissa," Tony said calmly, taking a sick, perverse pleasure in Cole's poleaxed expression.

"My family and I were away. In Europe. We got home day before yesterday, and there was this, this *letter*…"

"Yeah. I got one, too."

Finally, olive-green eyes met Tony's. "She never told you?"

"Nope. Up until a couple weeks ago, I had no clue." Tony shoved his hands in his back pockets. "Your wife know?"

Cole blew out a soft, humorless laugh. "No. It was—"

"Save it. I really don't give a damn."

"It was a fling, that's all," the guy said anyway, more than a little desperation edging his words. "Lasted less than a month. For what it's worth, Rissa called it off."

"That supposed to make me feel better? Or you?"

Cole's eyes widened, then shifted back to Josie. "Do you know…?"

"If she's mine? Not yet. In the works, though."

"When will you—?"

"In a couple of days. Hey—wanna go halfsies on the lab fee?"

Angry, scared eyes shot to his. "Not funny."

"No, it's not. But then, neither is finding out the kid you had every reason to believe was yours might not be."

"It wasn't—"

"Supposed to happen? Yeah, I got that."

Now panic flooded the jerk's face. "Sarah—my wife—she can't find out about this. It would kill her—"

"Dad?" Claire yelled from the car. "Are you coming?"

"Yeah, baby, be right there." Tony turned back to Cole. "One question—do you *want* to know?" A long moment passed before the man finally nodded. "Then you got a card or something?" Tony said over the sensation of riding out a hurricane in a rowboat. "So I can get in touch with you," he added irritably when the guy gave him deer-in-headlights.

"Uh, yeah." He fumbled for his wallet, pulling out an

embossed business card which he handed over. "Call my cell, nobody answers that except me."

Tony stared at the card for a second, then blew out a breath that barely dented the nausea. "Look, your wife's not gonna hear about any of this from me. No skin off my nose. But if the baby does turn out to be yours...?"

"I don't know," Cole said softly. "I don't..." After sparing Tony a final, helpless look, he ducked back into his fancy little car and sped off.

"Dad?" Claire asked, worried, when Tony and Josie reached the Volvo again. "Who was that?"

He caught the concern in Lili's eyes before he smiled at his daughter. "Somebody I went to school with," he said, swinging the baby into her car seat. "Guess he decided we should catch up with each other. Okay..." Josie strapped in, he clapped his hands. "Let's get this show on the road!"

As kids and dogs piled in, Lili looked at him over the car's roof and mouthed, "You okay?"

"Depends on what you mean by 'okay'," Tony muttered, sliding behind the wheel, taking a moment to steady his breathing. Soft, strong fingers briefly squeezed his knee, but he knew better than to look over. Knew in any case she wouldn't be looking at him, either. Instead, he yanked the shift into Reverse and backed out of his driveway.

"You know," he said quietly a few minutes later, when the kids were making such a racket they couldn't've heard fighter jets go over, "if you'd gotten here on time—"

"He would have missed you. I know."

Desperate to change the subject, Tony glanced over. "What was that sudden trip to the drugstore all about, anyway?"

"Just, um, needed some personal things," she said, giving him an embarrassed please-don't-make-me-spell-it-out look.

"Oh. Sorry," Tony muttered, wondering if a denser human being ever walked the planet.

Chapter Nine

Chasing a giggling, barefoot Josie around his room at the inn, taking things away as fast as she could grab them, Tony barely heard the soft knock. "Yeah, it's open—"

"Mine?" Josie said, clutching the faded, antique-looking doll, eyes wide.

"No, baby, it belongs to the people who live here—"

"Lili!" Still holding the doll hostage, she ran over on her chunky little legs and thrust the doll in Lili's face. "Pretty dolly!"

"Oooh, very pretty." Lili glanced at the crib set up on the other side of the spacious room, where Tony had already dumped Josie's favorite "friends." "But…" She crossed to the crib, snatching one of them out of it. "What about…?" She looked to Tony, holding up the goofy, long-legged bird.

"Harvey."

"Haavey," she said, imitating his accent so perfectly Tony

had to smile. "Harvey thinks you forgot him," she said, pulling a comically sad face, then hugging the bird to her. "He's sad, he wants his JoJo."

Josie looked skeptical for a moment, then dumped the doll on the floor and reached for her toy, roughly stroking him. "It's okay, Harvey," she said, her pronunciation the same as Tony's. "Don't be scared, I'm here." She yawned. And screwed her palm into one eye. "I won't leave you."

Tony's breath caught, before he dared to meet Lili's eyes. Eyes filled with caring so deep, so genuine, he had to look away.

"Your room okay?" he said, hauling his sleepy girl up into his arms.

"It's lovely, yes. The whole inn's beautiful. And it's so peaceful up here. Now I'm really glad I came. Where are the other girls?"

"Daph's off playing with Violet's boys, and I'm pretty sure Claire's with Stacey. And this little critter," he said, blowing a kiss into her neck, "needs to take her nap."

"No," she said, giggling, trying to wriggle free. "Don't want nap! Not s'eepy."

Tony swung her up and over the railing, gently plunking her into the crib. "Then you can have a nice, quiet rest with your friends, how's that?"

But the baby clung to the crib rail, her large, watery eyes darting around the strange room. A moment later her arms shot up, her face crumpled. "Don't wanna stay here! Wanna go wif you!"

"Okay, how about..." Tony looked over at Lili, then nodded toward the door between his room and the girls'. Her eyes following his, she nodded back. "Lili and I are gonna be right in here," he said, walking over and pushing open the door so she could see the other room. "I'll sit in that chair, okay? So you can see me?"

That got a skeptical look, followed by an even more skeptical, "P'omise?"

"Promise."

Arms shot up again. "Hug?"

Tony obliged, ignoring the pain, the fear, as the little girl whispered, "Love you," against his cheek.

"Love you, too, cupcake." Finally, a very wobbly Josie laid down on her side, Harvey safely tucked against her chest and eagle eyes pinned to where Tony said he'd be. Except even before they left, the eagle eyes were at half-mast.

"She'll be out in less than a minute," Tony whispered as he ushered Lili into the other room. Feeling like he was about to suffocate, he raised both windows, then opened the door to the hallway, letting in a welcome breeze. Then, with a weary sigh, he sank into one of the red plaid chairs. Lili lowered herself onto the edge of the nearest Colonial-spreaded twin bed, her gaze intense.

"So what happened?" she asked quietly, since obviously there'd been no opportunity to talk about his face-to-face with Cole before this. "And why are you looking at me like that?"

Because the four hours between the drive and lunch and getting settled in had given Tony lots of time to reconsider the wisdom of constantly unloading on the woman. "I don't get it. Why you care so much. It's not like you have a personal stake in any of this or anything."

Several seconds passed before she said, with some heat, "You know…if you think I'm being nosy, just say so."

"No, it's not that—"

"Then I *care* because I just do. About all of you. That *is* the stake I have in this. So deal with it."

Somehow, that didn't help. But Tony replayed the conversation, anyway, even as he realized it didn't sound any better out loud than it had the previous hundred times it had repeated itself in his brain.

"Do you think Cole would even want Josie?" Lili asked when he'd finished.

"I have no idea, to tell you the truth. But he didn't exactly lie across the driveway so we couldn't leave, either." Tony pushed himself out of the too-soft chair to pace the room, idly picking up assorted items from Daphne's exploded gym bag and setting them on the bed where she'd already set her favorite ball-gowned Barbie against the pillows. The contents of Claire's bag, on the other hand, were—he opened a bureau drawer and smiled—already neatly installed in their temporary quarters. "I'm guessing he doesn't know, himself," he said, shutting the drawer, then turning to Lili. "Although if you want my take on it, what has him scared spitless is his wife finding out."

"But he does want to know the results?"

"So he said."

"So what does this mean?"

"I don't know what it *means,* okay?" Tony said, finally giving in to the hopeless, helpless fury he'd been holding back all morning. His gaze swung to the baby, now out like a light in the other room, and his heart hurt with loving her. With the sick fear that he might lose her, that the test would say he wasn't her father and Cole Jamison would get over himself and tell his wife and they'd decide it was okay, they'd work it out, Josie could come live with them—

"It's like everybody expects me to be in charge," he said, his voice strained as he leaned one wrist against the door-frame, staring at his little girl, "to know what I'm doing. Only every damn day somebody decides to change the freaking rules." He swallowed past the golf ball in his throat. "I'll do anything to protect my babies, Lil. But it's like every day I know less and less how I'm supposed to do that."

Tony hardly reacted at first when Lili's arms wrapped around his waist from behind, her hands pressing into heart as her cheek did against his spine. Then he tensed, dreading the shushes, the crap variations on "It'll be okay, you'll see." They never came. Instead she simply held him, held tight, then tighter still, until his breathing got back to something like regular again and the vicious red haze cleared from his eyes.

Releasing a long, shaky breath, he curled the fingers of his free hand around one of hers. "I'm okay now."

He felt her head lift. "Are you sure?"

"Yeah."

But even as her arms slipped away, Tony turned, seeing again that refuge in her eyes he knew he was in no place to accept, no matter how desperately he wanted it. Saw, too, something else, something that blotted out reason but good, something that brought his hands up to her shoulders and his mouth down on hers, that sucked in her brief gasp of surprise and kept on going, like by kissing her he could somehow glean a little taste of sanity in the midst of all this chaos. Then her hands were on his back, strong hands from all the scrubbing and dough-rolling, kneading rock-hard muscles through his T-shirt as her mouth opened under his and the kiss became like a freaking runaway train, totally outta control, a rush to end all rushes, and he thought, briefly, *Definitely not little Lili anymore—*

Then reason tapped Tony on the shoulder and cleared its throat, and the train derailed. His hands still clamped on Lili's shoulders, Tony broke the kiss, seeing confusion in her eyes that must've mirrored his own.

"Sorry," he muttered, looking away.

"For…?"

He forced his gaze back to hers. "You're kidding, right?"

"It was just a kiss, Tony—"

"*Just* a kiss? *Just* a kiss? Jeez, honey—if that's what you consider *just* a kiss, I'm almost afraid to think what you'd call *spectacular.*" He pivoted, raking his hand through his hair. "In any case, I haven't kissed another woman since Rissa—"

His wife's name caught in his throat, like a bite of something gone down the wrong way.

"Yes, I'd rather imagined that was the case."

He turned back. Caught the insane blush he'd apparently missed the first time, a blush at total odds with the way she was standing there, all calm and collected. Strange woman.

Strange, incredible woman.

"I, uh…" He nodded toward the other room. "Need to stick around, in case JoJo wakes up. You mind keepin' an eye on the other girls until we come down?"

Her gaze unwavering, Lili shook her head. "Of course not. Maybe you can get some rest, as well. With everything going on—"

"Yeah, that's a good idea," Tony said, walking her to the door. Deliberately not touching her. Making himself crazier than he already was. "See ya later, then."

"Undoubtedly," she said with a small smile stretching slightly swollen lips, then left.

Tony shut the door behind her and walked back into his own room, sinking onto the edge of the double bed with his face in his hands, thinking, *Good goin', bonehead.*

He lifted his eyes to stare at his own tight smile in the dresser mirror in front of him. Kissing the woman had been dumb enough. Kissing her in front of an open door?

In a house full of kids?

Somebody sure as hell was looking out for his sorry ass, that's all he had to say.

Daphne crashed through the back door and out into the big backyard, breathing so hard her chest hurt. Both dogs ran at her, barking and jumping; she pushed right through them and kept going, not stopping until she reached the very back, practically throwing herself through the tire swing hanging from the biggest tree she'd ever seen. The tire smelled funny, and the way it bounced made her tummy feel kind of icky for a second, but then she dug her feet into the dirt and twisted the swing all up and let go, spinning and spinning and spinning in a cloud of dust, the dogs and the trees and George and Zeke running from the house toward her a great big blur, like maybe she could spin what she'd just seen out of her head…

"You gonna barf?" Zeke asked when she stopped, feeling like her eyes wouldn't stay still. Zeke was six, only a year younger than her, so she was better friends with him than she was with George, who was almost eleven.

She shook her head. "Uh-uh," she said, then twisted herself up again. "I make myself dizzy lots. It's fun—"

She'd just gone up to her room to get some fruit rolls out of her backpack to share with the boys. Except when she'd gotten to the door, there were Daddy and Lili—

Again, the world spun, faster and faster and faster, until the boys stopped the swing, jerking her back. George was looking at her funny, his face all serious underneath his orange hair. "You okay?"

Daphne wriggled back out of the swing, swiping at a smudge of dirt across her pink T-shirt. It didn't come off. She shrugged, tucking the secret deeper inside her, where she could turn it over and over in her mind until she decided what to do with it. How she felt about it. Right now, though, she felt kinda fizzy inside, like when they'd watch the Macy's parade on TV while the Thanksgiving turkey was cooking at Nana's, and Daphne knew that meant Christmas was *finally* coming. Which of course made her feel sad about Mom, and how weird last Thanksgiving and Christmas were without her—

"Yeah, sure," she said, pushing the sad thought away. "Hey, wanna play hide-and-seek? I'll count." She turned to the tree and covered her eyes. "One…two…three…"

Behind her, she heard the boys and the dogs all run off. Still counting, Daphne uncovered her eyes and leaned her forehead against the tree, wondering why, if she wasn't dizzy anymore, everything still seemed to be spinning.

Lifting her head, she called out, "Ready or not, here I come!"

The next morning Lili followed her nose to the sunlight-flooded kitchen, all yellows and creams and touches of red, where Violet was mixing up batter of some kind in a large ceramic bowl and dogs roamed, hopeful. While Ed stood sentry over the proceedings, Simon—best described as a living haystack—plodded over to give Lili a quick schlurp with his tongue.

"Simon! How many times have I told you, don't lick the guests?"

"It's okay," Lili said. Eyeing the coffeemaker.

Violet grinned. "Help yourself. Mugs're right in the cupboard." She measured out a half cup of sugar, dumped it into the batter. "Another early riser, huh?"

"I like the quiet," Lili said, hugging her coffee to her as she settled at the table.

"Lord, me, too."

"Anything I can to help?"

"Nah, just pullin' everything together so I'm ready to go when the rest of 'em haul their lazy butts out of bed. Figured I'd do waffles. Everybody likes waffles, right?"

She set the bowl on the back of the stove—"Damn dog loves waffle batter, go figure"—pulled down a large skillet from an overhead rack and clanged it on the stove, then poured her own coffee.

"Let's go sit outside. Enjoy the peace while it lasts."

The back porch off the kitchen faced a yard with so many trees it looked like a park, through which Lili caught a glimpse of mountains, gilded by the morning sun. A warm breeze danced through a million leaves, the sound so soothing she closed her eyes, savoring. Violet chuckled softly.

"Yeah. It's like that," she said, smiling when Lili opened her eyes again. "I'm glad you guys could get up here."

"Me, too." She took a sip of the strong, rich coffee. "Was this always your house?"

"Oh, God, no," Violet said with a cross between a laugh and a snort. "Although it's been part of my life since I was a kid."

"Sounds intriguing."

"That's one way of putting it. My mother usedta work here, as a maid, so I did, too, in the summers before I got married." Her mouth flattened. "The first time. When my first husband left me and the boys, Doris—she's the former owner—took us in, in exchange for me helpin' her after her husband died. She promised to leave the inn to me, only when she died, there wasn't a will, and her daughter sold the place." She lifted her mug. "To Rudy."

"Oh, dear," Lili said, and Violet shrugged. Then she smiled, holding her jumble of orange curls off her face.

"Only when Rudy found out? I think he felt worse than I did. So he invited the boys and me to come live here, anyway, help him out while he was fixing the place up…and then, when he was movin' furniture around in Doris's old room? Damned if he didn't find the will." She leaned back, resting her feet on one of the empty chairs. "Funny thing— if he hadn't've told me, I would've never known."

"But he did?"

"Yeah," she said on a wondering sigh, then looked at Lili, a half smile pulling at her mouth. "He did." She faced front again. "The lawyer said easiest thing would be to go in as partners. So we did. In more ways than one." She took a sip of her coffee, not looking at Lili. "So what's goin' on between you and Tony?"

Lili's own mouthful went down the wrong way. "Isn't that a little personal?" she said when she stopped coughing.

"Hmm…I'm guessing you didn't notice the beard burn before you came downstairs yesterday?" When Lili's hand flew to her cheek, Violet chuckled. "But it's okay, I don't think anybody else did, either. Except me, of course."

"There's nothing going on," Lili said quietly, intent on those the mountains. "Not of any significance, anyway."

"Got it," Violet said, only to then add, "You know what's botherin' Tony?"

Lili's eyes cut to Violet's. "Bothering him?"

"Yeah. Rudy and me, we were talkin' about it last night, after you guys all went to bed. Tony seems, I dunno. Not like he's sad or grieving, but like he's…worried or something."

"He just has his hands full," Lili said, hiding once more behind her mug, "with the girls and everything."

Although she found Violet's slight squint unnerving, it wasn't Lili's place to divulge that Tony was waiting for a phone call that could quite possibly shatter his world. Even more than it had already been.

"So what's next for you after you go back to Hungary?"

At that, a clammy feeling came over her. "I'm not sure." She smiled, although it was an effort. "Figure out what I'm supposed to be doing with my life, I suppose."

"Yeah, been there," Violet said on a sigh, then fell quiet for a moment. "You know, I read this article once somewhere where you were asked to name the last five winners of a bunch of important awards, like the Oscars and Nobel Peace Prizes, stuff like that. People at the top of their games, you know? Then you were asked to name the five people who'd meant the most to *you* during your lifetime. A lot easier to come up with that last list, huh?"

Lili smiled. "Definitely."

Violet twisted in her chair. "When I was a kid, I useta

dream about doing something important one day. Not necessarily being famous, just bein'…somebody. And here I am," she said, waving her mug at the scene in front of her, "reconciled to the fact that I'm never gonna find a cure for any disease, or solve the energy crisis, or win a gold medal. But ya know, what I do here, providing a haven for people who're maybe looking for a few stress-free days…I think that's important. Being there for my kids, for Rudy… they'll remember that. We all have our place, our purpose. It's not what you do, it's how much of *you* you put into it, right—?"

"Hey," Rudy said, filling the doorway. "I don't pay you to sit around and drink coffee all day."

Unperturbed, Violet grinned at Lili. "Isn't he cute?" she said, then faced her husband, chin cradled in hand. "Since you don't *pay* me anything, looks to me like you don't have a lot of say in the matter."

"Yeah, well, there's a buncha hungry people millin' around in your kitchen, wondering what happened to the cook."

Violet shrugged, doing an exaggerated yawn and stretch before finally hauling herself out of the chair, yelping slightly when Rudy lightly smacked her behind as she passed him.

"So hard to find good help these days," Rudy said, wagging his head as he gallantly held out one arm to usher Lili back into the kitchen, where her gaze immediately latched onto Tony, Josie in his arms, arrowing through the swarm of small Vaccaros toward the coffeemaker. Although he'd obviously just showered and shaved, the pouches underneath his eyes and creases bracketing his mouth—as well as the slight wince at Zeke's shriek of laughter when Ed jumped up to give him a kiss—spoke of a man who had not slept well.

This is not your problem to fix, Lili thought, again, turning away to smile for Daphne, already seated at the extra-large kitchen table, her face already dirty. Then she briefly caught Tony's eyes and realized what day it was, that the poor man must have felt as if his cell phone was a time bomb.

"Hey," Rudy said as the room filled with the spicy scent of sizzling sausages, "weather says it's not gonna be too hot today. So who's up for a hike later? There's some great trails around here. And it's been months since I've been able to go traipsing through the woods with my kids. Tony?"

"Sure, sounds great," he said with a fleeting smile as he strapped Josie into a high chair. "And no groaning from you guys," he said to the girls, who looked less than thrilled with the prospect. "It'll do us good, to get outside. Commune with nature."

Daphne shrugged, but Claire looked as if she'd been consigned to clean latrines for the next six months. Then Stacey, Rudy's teenage daughter, said she wasn't feeling well and would he mind if she begged off, which of course gave Claire the excuse she needed not to go, and then Violet said a new cleaning lady was coming so *she* couldn't go and besides somebody needed to stay with Josie, right?

Rudy crossed his huge arms over his chest. "Does *anybody* wanna go with me?" he said, sounding so bereft Lili laughed.

"You've still got the boys, and Daph. And Tony and me." Simon woofed behind Ed, who spun around in place three times before joining in. Ed, Lili had already learned, was always up for an adventure. "And the dogs."

"Forget it," Violet said, carting a plate stacked with waffles to the table. "Last time this *thing*," she said, nudging Simon out of the way with her knee, "went on a walk with you, it took me a week to get all the burrs off him. Only way he goes is if you shave 'im or make 'im wear a wet suit."

"Party pooper," Rudy said amidst a chorus of giggles from the table as the kids watched the exchange. Especially when Simon dropped to a lying position to watch Violet's comings and goings, his expression baleful through drooping, spiky eyebrows.

What a simple, rich life Rudy and Violet had made for themselves and their kids, Lili thought, her gaze drifting to Tony, patiently feeding a two-year-old. Why wouldn't that be enough?

"Actually," Claire suddenly piped up, "maybe I will go."

Tony glanced at his daughter, relief evident in his smile. "Glad you decided to grace us with your presence," he said, his gentle teasing filled with nothing but love for his prickly, moody child.

Then Claire's gaze swung to Lili, once more laced with so much wariness she felt the ridiculous sting of tears, as if she were a child herself. She'd thought they'd moved past that—

Oh, dear God—had Claire seen them kiss?

Except they'd all spent the rest of the day together yesterday. Surely the child would have said something if she'd seen them? She certainly didn't seem to have any qualms about speaking up otherwise. So, no, Lili decided, relaxing slightly. Whatever that look had been about, she sincerely doubted the kiss was the culprit.

Then she reminded herself…what did it matter, anyway, whether Claire liked her or not? Wanted her company or not? Trusted her or not? Perhaps, in another world—a world where little girls who'd just lost a parent didn't resent anyone attempting to take that parent's place—she might have reason to indulge a few fairy-tale fantasies, of being what this broken family needed. What Tony needed.

But Lili knew better than anyone that a child's unconditional love wasn't interchangeable. From everything she could gather, Marissa had been a good mother, the kind of mother whose death leaves a gaping hole in her children's hearts.

The kind of woman, she thought, stealing another glance

at Tony, whose betrayal leaves another kind of hole, even deeper and wider. A hole only a fool would attempt to fill.

Whatever her purpose was, being with Tony and his daughters wasn't it.

Hardly a revelation, of course. But for some reason the message seemed to register this time. Oddly, though, instead of making her sad, Lili felt suddenly free. Free to simply enjoy the moment, free to offer whatever comfort and support she could to Tony without endangering her own peace of mind.

Free to love him without all those pesky expectations and hopes and worries about reciprocation.

She dug into her waffles and sausages with more enthusiasm than she'd felt for anything in weeks.

If Tony'd thought a hike was somehow gonna take his mind off the dreaded phone call—not to mention unrelenting replays of that anything-but-*just*-a-kiss—he'd been wrong on both counts. Although on some level, he could at least appreciate how pretty it was up here, the blue skies and the yakkety-yakking brook and the blinding sunlight—

Okay, so maybe he wasn't exactly in the right mood for this.

At least the girls, far enough ahead with the others that the forest would occasionally swallow them up, seemed to be having a good enough time. Daph was, anyway. As usual. Because Daph was made of rubber—everything bounced off her or she, it. Like him, though, Claire was there in body but not at all in spirit, tramping dutifully along behind the boys, looking like she'd rather have a cavity filled.

"I cannot tell you how much I empathize with her," Lili said a couple of feet away, making Tony start. There was something different about her this morning, but damned if he could put a finger on it. Not that she was moody or anything. But then that was the thing about Lil, she never seemed to get pissy for no good reason. Of course, the real test was toleratin' each other for the long haul—

"In what way?" he said, removing his head from his butt.

"Feeling a bit like an alien life form, desperately wanting to be part of the human race."

"You should say that to her."

"I did, as it happens. The other day, when we were making the dumplings." She smiled. "When she giggled." Then the smile faded. "Now she's back to looking at me as though I have fleas."

"You do realize she looks at everyone like that?"

"I suppose I did, too, at that age. And well beyond."

"You? A pain in the butt?"

"Hard to believe, I know." Her eyes flicked to his, then scampered away. "For a while I thought perhaps she, um, saw us." Her cheeks reddened. "Yesterday. In their room."

"I sincerely doubt it," Tony said, his own face prickling as well. "Claire's not exactly one for keepin' secrets—"

"Hey, guys," Rudy yelled back. "There's a falls up ahead, if you'd like to stop and rest for a minute. The kids can go wading!"

"Just make sure Daph takes her shoes off first," Tony called back, even as he realized something was building in his brain, something about to come crashing out of his mouth, and he had like exactly one second to stomp on it or—

"You know that jerk you were gonna marry?"

Lili stumbled over a tree root, righting herself before Tony could grab for her. "I used to know him quite well," she said, deadpan. "What about him?"

"If it'd been me? I would have lived with *Godzilla's* mother if it meant getting to kiss you on a regular basis."

She stood, frozen, for several seconds before starting forward again. "It wasn't *that* good," she mumbled.

"Uh, yeah, it was. I can't imagine what—"

Okay, he could stop right there. Had damn sight *better* stop right there.

"You can't imagine…?"

"Never mind."

He heard a huff. "And one of the few things that *really* annoys me is people who don't finish their sentences."

"Fine," he said, turning. "I can't imagine, if you kiss like that? What you must be like in bed. And don't look at me like that, you asked."

She blinked at him for several seconds, then started walking again. "I think this is one of those places we're not supposed to go?"

"Hey. I'm a guy. We're always at that particular place. And anyway, I tried to stop. You wouldn't let me."

Silence dropped between them like a giant army boot. They hiked another fifty feet or so in that throbbing quiet— except for the deafening chatter of roughly five bazillion birds—until they reached the falls. The boys and Daphne were already in the water at the base of the falls while Claire hung back, too cool for school. Although even Claire looked impressed by the scene. As well she should.

Tony tilted back the brim of his ball cap, trying to take it all in. Grumpy as he was, he still had to admit it was like something right out of a freaking travel brochure. They weren't talking Niagara or anything, maybe a twenty-foot drop, but between the trees soaring all around them, the gurgling stream tumbling over and around glistening black rocks, the water sparkling from the spears of sunlight cutting right through all those trees…it was something else.

"Wow," Tony said at the same time Lili said, so softly he almost didn't catch it, "I have no idea what I'd be like in bed. I'm a virgin."

Chapter Ten

And you told him this, why?

Staring at the roaring waterfall, Lili felt Tony's gaze bore through her. Certainly, it wasn't any of his business. Nor did her sexual experience have the slightest bearing on their relationship. And yet, his comment had provoked something inside her, shoving the words out of her mouth.

"That's a joke, right?"

Her brow knotted, she looked at him, only to nearly laugh at his incredulous expression. "Not at all."

"But…you said you were engaged…?"

"Peter was very old-fashioned. And I was still quite young."

"Excuse me, but Peter must've been *dead*. And that was how many years ago?"

Facing the falls again, Lili shoved her hands her shorts pockets. "You know, when I told you about taking care of my mother, I said it was my own choice? Well, this falls into the same category. Until Peter, I'd never met anyone I cared to take my clothes off for. When he didn't seem particularly interested whether I did or not…"

"You were scarred for life, what?"

She softly laughed. "Of course not. But neither did I see that…misstep as an excuse to *lower* my standards, either." Looking back at Tony, she said, "It's not as if I took some vow of chastity, or had any deep-seated fears about sex, or any of that. I simply wanted to be *in* love when I *made* love."

"It can't be that simple."

"Why not? Sex for its own sake has never interested me." She paused, took a deep breath. "And until recently, I've never felt I was particularly missing out."

Lili could feel Tony's eyes on her face again, knew he was much too smart to not get her point. Granted, there'd probably be scant opportunity while they were here to use any of the condoms from that last-minute trip to the drugstore, but her buying them certainly spoke to a major shift in her thinking. And heaven knows hope had flared, however briefly, with that not-to-be-believed kiss, when she'd felt more than ample evidence of Tony's interest in taking things further. At least physically.

But then, as she'd said, she wasn't naïve. Simply because *she* didn't/couldn't/refused to separate sex from love, she was well aware the same wasn't true for the vast majority of the human population. Especially the male half. After all, an erection was only an instinct-driven response to physical stimulus—

Tony's ringtone startled her out of her thoughts. He yanked the phone off his belt as though flames were shooting from it, only to simply stare at the display, letting it ring.

"Tony?"

"It's them."

"Answer it," Lili said softly.

Finally, he lifted the phone to his ear. "Hello?…Yeah, this is him." Expressionless, he faced slightly away; Lily watched, barely breathing, her heart cracking when his head dropped forward, his eyes squeezed shut. "Yeah," he mumbled after a moment, looking up. "I'll do that. Thanks."

For several seconds, he stood still, staring blankly at his other children, Daphne laughing and splashing in the water, Claire sitting on the edge of the stream, hugging her knees as though trying to hold herself, and her life, together.

"Tony?" Lili whispered, tears stinging.

"You mind leavin' me alone for a sec?" His voice…it didn't even sound like Tony. And it killed her, watching him refuse to cower under yet another blow, helpless to do a single thing to comfort him. Not that there were any words. But at the moment she didn't dare even lay a hand on his arm without arousing suspicion.

"Of course not. Do you…I think we should probably head back home, don't you?"

At last he shifted his gaze to hers. There was nothing there. Nothing. No pain, no anger, certainly no real comprehension. But far worse than that, there was no Tony. However, even as fear rippled through her, he took a deep breath, gave her a small smile. "I'll let you know."

She left him then, to pick her way down the slippery bank to the stream's edge, where both Rudy and Claire shot her questioning glances which she didn't return. Instead she forced herself to join in the children's play, even removing her shoes and socks to wade in the freezing water. Her heart, however, stayed with the man on the other side of the stream, his eyes fixed on them…but his mind, Lili suspected, was very, very far away indeed.

Even numb with shock, Tony realized he needed to pull himself together, pronto. Not if he didn't want a buttload of unwanted questions to come crashing down on his head. So after a minute or two, like he'd already done God knew how many times over the past year—okay, longer, ever since he and Rissa started having problems—he got up off his sorry ass, plastered a smile to his face and acted like everything was okay.

Never mind that all he wanted to do was go straight back to the inn, haul Josie into his arms and hold on for dear life…followed by wanting to punch something until his knuckles were bloody.

Naturally Claire got to him first, her little pinched face and concerned eyes getting to him in other, far more painful ways. He preempted the inevitable interrogation, though, by plunking down on the damp ground beside her to remove his shoes and socks.

"You're not actually going in there?"

Thank you, Diversionary Tactic #356.

"I actually am. Everybody else is. Except you. Look, even Lili's in the water," he said, and she looked over and waved, and he suddenly remembered their conversation before The Phone Call, that she'd never had sex, a conversation that seemed blurry and faded and irrelevant, now that he knew for sure—

Tony doubled over, using the excuse to stuff his socks into his shoes as a cover for feeling like he'd just been gutted. He'd thought the *not* knowing was horrible? This was a hundred, a thousand times worse.

Steeling himself, Tony got up to carefully wade into the icy stream, the sharp sting of cold making him catch his breath, making him wish it would go right through his bloodstream to freeze his heart so he couldn't feel the pain. Lili's eyes glanced off his before just before Daphne splashed her; she gasped, then spun around to grab the giggling seven-year-old in her arms, and Tony's heart ached ever harder, at how messed up everything was.

Everything.

I can't make everybody happy, dammit! he wanted to scream, his head pounding as he thought how fathers were a lot like doctors—even if they couldn't fix things, they shouldn't make things worse, either.

Somehow, he got through the rest of the morning, and the walk back, and lunch, sticking closer to the kids than usual, until Violet gathered up all the females and took them to the outlet mall and Rudy went off somewhere with the boys, leaving Tony with Josie and the dogs.

And the looming prospect of making the worst phone call of his life.

By the time they hit up the third store, Lili could feel her poor credit card trembling deep in her purse, whimpering, "Please! No more! I'll do whatever you want, just please stop swiping me through those machines!"

Blithely ignoring the plastic's pleas, she surveyed the acres of pretties before her. Who knew a simple holiday in New Hampshire would release a latent desire to shore up the sagging U.S. economy?

Not to mention her sagging spirits. Although there'd been far too much laughter and loud music and chatter in the car on the way here for Lili to obsess about Tony's plight, it still murmured in the back of her brain, a white noise that was anything but soothing. The good news was, however, that the expedition had seemed to perk Claire up a bit, as well, even if she'd spent all the cash her father had given her on things for Josie, rather than herself. But while Lili still caught the occasional wary look, she also noticed the girl seemed to stick closer to Lili than the others.

Interesting.

Now, as Stacey led Violet straight to Juniors, Lili took Daphne's hand and gave her a stern look. "Okay, cutie—last store. It's now or never."

"But I can't decide," Miss Dimples said, clearly determined to take *her* cash—currently keeping Lili's whimpering credit card company—to the grave.

"Yeah," Claire said as, for the third time, she looked longingly at the racks of clothes. "We just went shopping with Nana, it's not like we really *need* anything."

"Oh, yeah—khaki jumpers and white polo shirts, whoo-hoo," Lili said, leading them smartly toward the Girls' section, figuring if indulgent auntie was the only role she was allowed in this little scenario, she would play it to the hilt.

"And blue sweaters," Daphne put in.

"Oh, well, then," Lili said, and Daph giggled.

"Besides," Claire said, moving toward a table of embroidered, beaded hoodies in assorted shades of blindingly bright, "I already spent all my money on the baby." Lili watched as the girl delicately traced one finger over a silky curlicue; Daph, too, grabbed one of the hoodies, holding it up to her for a second before yanking it on. Two sizes too big, it came halfway down her thighs. And looked absolutely adorable.

"This is so cool!" she said, her dark curls spilling over the hot pink fabric.

"You should totally get it, Daph," Claire said, nodding. And tucking her hand behind her back. "It's really pretty."

The smaller girl frowned at the price tag. "Do I have enough money?"

Claire checked. "Plenty," she said, the torn look in her eyes speaking volumes—that she wanted, but for whatever reason thought she couldn't, or shouldn't have. Now Lili wondered if Claire's insistence on buying toys and outfits for Josie had been a thinly veiled diversionary tactic so she wouldn't have to deal with the inevitable body issues that arose when buying clothes for herself.

Well, that's just crazy, Lili thought, marching over to the table and skimming the choices. "Which is your favorite

color, Claire? Red? Orange? Oh—how about this turquoise?" she said, yanking it off the pile and unfolding it,
the dark pink and purple embroidery and beads shimmering in the store's lights, and for a brief moment she was
twelve again, watching her mother pour herself into a
spangly, sparkly costume Lili would never wear. "What do
you think, Daph? Wouldn't this be perfect with Claire's
hair color?"

"Yeah, totally. Try it on, Claire—"

"Oh, no, I don't think so—"

"Just so I can see how it looks on you. Because I think…"
Lili scanned the pile for one large enough to fit her. Bright
yellow. With turquoise and purple embroidery. Toss in a pair
of wings and she could hide out in the rainforest. "I'm going
to get this one," she said, tugging it over her head.

Finally Claire put hers on, too. "Wow, it's…big."

"That's the style," Lili said. "Hey—now we all look like
Hollis!"

Daphne giggled and even Claire grinned, walking a few
feet away to admire her reflection in a mirror. "Except Hollis
wouldn't be caught dead in beads."

"Another reason why it's good to be a girl. Right, Daph?"

"Yeah," she said, fist-pumping—

"But I spent all my money already," Claire said.

"Oh, this is my treat. For you, too, Daphne."

"Thanks!"

"Really?" Claire said, still looking at her reflection.

"Really."

"Holy bejeebers!" Violet called across the store at them,
shielding her eyes with her hand. "Those bright enough?
They'll be able to see the three of ya in Canada!"

Lili and the girls all burst out laughing, then removed the
tops so Lili could pay for them. As they carted them to the
cashier, Daphne said, "Nana's going to *totally* hate these."

Prying the quaking credit card from her wallet, Lili glanced at Claire. Who shrugged. "She'll live."

At least this, Lili thought, handing everything to the girl behind the register as the worries she'd held off all afternoon about Tony and Josie roared back, flooding her heart.

Josie down for her nap, Tony and the dogs went out onto the empty front porch. Buoyed by the beasts' silent *Go on, man—you can do this* expressions, he dragged Cole Jamison's business card out of his wallet, punching in the number before he lost his nerve. Cole picked up on the first ring.

"Jamison here…. Hello? Is anybody th—"

"She's not mine."

Cole sucked in a breath. "They're sure?"

"They do a double test. So, yeah. They're sure."

A pause. "Still doesn't mean I'm the father."

"Excuse me?"

"Without *my* DNA, there's no way of proving the kid's mine."

Dropping onto a wicker chair by the front door, Tony rubbed his eyes, trying to make the pieces of this ridiculous puzzle fit. "Look, you idiot," he said softly, "it's not like I *wanted* the test to turn out this way. I mean, I should be happy as hell that you obviously don't want her. But if Rissa sent you a letter, too, I assume that kinda narrows it down—"

"And who's to say you and I were the only chumps to get letters?"

Tony shot to his feet, even though he couldn't punch out the guy's lights through the phone. More's the pity. "And maybe this isn't about us, it's about Josie—"

"You can't force me to get a test, Vaccaro. And since *you* obviously don't want to give her up…" He heard a sigh. "I'm just trying to make this easier for everyone. My wife, my kids…they can't find out about this."

Tony almost laughed. "Yeah, well, maybe you should've thought that through a little harder three years ago. You really are a piece of work, aren'tcha? Although not a very bright one, since you kinda outted yourself when you showed up at my house."

"I panicked, okay? I didn't know what she'd told you, didn't want you coming to *my* house—"

"Yeah, I got that. And the thing is, we *don't* know if she told anybody else." Tony blew out a sharp breath. "Which means there's a real strong possibility this is gonna come back to bite one or both of us in the butt one day. No, I can't force you to take a paternity test. And yeah, in the short term it would definitely be in my best interests if you didn't. But neither do I want this hangin' over my head for the next however many years, wondering if and when you're gonna suddenly have a change of heart—"

"That won't—"

"And if God forbid something happened to Josie and I couldn't donate bone marrow or whatever because I'm not the kid's father, you better believe at that point? I *would* hunt you down and get a piece of your hair or a chunk outta your backside, it wouldn't matter to me, and get that proof. And *then* I'd go in and get whatever it was Josie needed!"

"You're insane."

"Yeah, like that frightens me. So you think about it. In any case, you don't wanna contest the fact that my name's on her birth certificate, then you send me some sort of affidavit to that effect, giving me full and permanent custody."

"Then you have to swear not to tell her about me."

"Ever? You know I can't do that."

"Then no deal," Cole said, and hung up.

As Tony sat there, softly banging the phone against his forehead, he heard the screen door open, saw out of the corner of his eye Rudy come out onto the porch.

"Where're the boys?" Tony asked.

"In their room, playing some video game." He crossed to the railing, leaned against it. "Wanna share?" the big dude asked quietly, folding his arms over a white T-shirt probably a size smaller than it should've been.

Tony's mouth pulled tight. "How much did you hear?"

"Enough to wanna smack you upside the head for not sayin' anything." Those weird blue eyes seared right through him. "Rissa *cheated* on you?"

Leave it to Rudy to not mince words. "Yeah. I didn't find out until a few weeks ago. The day of the party, actually." He filled Rudy in on the few details he had—although he left Cole's name out if it, for the moment—then sagged back in the chair, spent.

Rudy muttered a choice word, then shook his head. "Violet swore something was off, but I figured what does she know, the two of you have only met a cuppla times. Today, though, up at the falls? Hate to tell ya, but you were doing a damn lousy job of hiding your feelings."

"Thanks."

"No problem. But let me guess—nobody else knows, either."

"No. Well, Lili. But that's…" *Another mess entirely.*

"What that is, is something else you suck at hiding your feelings about." When Tony's eyes shifted to his cousin's, the other man smirked. "And yes, it's that obvious."

Tony sighed. "She's…"

"Yeah, can't wait to hear how you're gonna finish that sentence."

"It doesn't matter how I finish that sentence—it's all the rest of it I can't finish!"

The words practically exploded in Tony's brain. Rudy's lips curved.

"Why? Because it's *too soon?* Or were you plannin' on waitin' twelve years like I did?"

"I wasn't *plannin'* on anything. I—" His lips pressed together, Tony leaned forward again. "If being with Rissa taught me anything, it's how much energy relationships take. You lose focus, you're screwed. With everything else goin' on in my life right now? Starting a relationship…not gonna happen. And why're you lookin' at me like that?"

"You honest to God think you're to blame for Rissa's havin' an affair?"

"You sound like Lili."

"Knew I liked that woman."

Tony almost smiled, then sighed again. "These things don't happen in a vacuum, Rudy—"

"And maybe your wife had issues that had nothin' to do with you." Rudy downright glowered at him. "We grew up together, Tone, I know you better than I know at least half my brothers. I watched you with the girls, watched you with Rissa…" Shaking his head, he looked away, his mouth set. "True, nobody knows what goes on inside a marriage except the two people involved. Hell, sometimes even *they* don't. But…" He faced Tony again. "Whatever reasons Marissa had for doing what she did? It wasn't you, Tone. It just wasn't."

Tony got to his feet, walking over to the top of the steps. Dark gray clouds had begun to slide in from the north; a damp breeze whipped through Tony's T-shirt, chilling his skin. "Whatever. It doesn't change anything. That I'm in no position to, to…"

"Get something goin' with Lili?"

"Yeah. Or no, in this case." He frowned at Rudy. "There's the kids, for one thing. And Rissa's parents, for another." Sighed, he looked out over the front yard. "Even if I was ready, they're not."

"Not so sure Daphne'd agree with you there," Rudy said, and Tony smiled.

"Just because she gets along with Lil doesn't mean she's ready to accept her as her mom. Claire wears all her emotions on the outside—I may not totally understand *what* she's feeling, but I always know *that* she's feeling. Daph, though…she's like me. Show must go on and all that crap."

Rudy chuckled. "Kids are bizarre, aren't they?" Then he said, "Okay, I know the timing sucks. But it just seems to me…" He crossed his arms high on his chest. "We both fell hard the first time, when we were too young to know what hit us. Sometimes that works out and sometimes that doesn't. But when things happen that early, that intensely, you don't realize for most people, it doesn't come that easy."

Grunting softly, he rubbed his bristly head. "Until suddenly you're alone again. Only, like you said , there's all this *stuff* in the way there wasn't the first time, most of which is all in here—" he tapped his temple "—all these expectations and anxieties and crap, and suddenly building a nuclear reactor seems easier than finding somebody to share your life with."

"But I'm not—"

"Shut up, I'm not done. Maybe you don't think you want or need somebody right now, or the kids can't deal, whatever. But let me tell you something—one day you're gonna wake up and realize you've done everything for everybody else and haven't done a damn thing for you, and you're gonna be pissed. *Especially* when it hits you what you let slip through your fingers—"

"And maybe you should just butt out, okay? I get what you're saying. I do. But right now, it's *not* about me. And even if…" Tony shoved out a breath. "I'm not sayin' there's not a spark. I'm not even sayin', if things were different, I wouldn't mind acting on that spark. But I gotta think about Lili, too, you know? She's just now getting back on her feet after all that time she spent with her mother, the last thing she needs is to get dragged into this craziness."

At the sound of Violet's minivan crunching down the gravel path, both men turned. A few seconds later, doors popped and slid open and females poured out, laden with bags. Naturally Tony's gaze swept over both his daughters first, but they settled on Lili, laughing about something with Violet as they brought up the rear, and she looked so…honest and real, with her don't-give-a-damn hair and kitty-wampus glasses. Then, still laughing, she looked up and their gazes caught, her smile faltering slightly, like she could read his mind.

Or maybe sort out the mess inside it. Because it was hard to look at her and feel her presence and not think about everything that Rudy'd said, not wonder if maybe she'd bring a little bit of normalcy to the craziness, maybe…

"Maybe," Rudy said quietly beside him, before the rest were close enough to hear, "you should give the woman the chance to make her own decisions." When Troy glared at him, he lifted his hands, smiling. "Just sayin'." Then he grinned for his daughter, stomping up the steps wearing a printed top with the designer name taking up most of the front.

"Huh. That's new."

"See?" she said, turning to Violet. "Told you he'd notice. Like it?" she said, twirling. "It's Tommy Hilfiger."

"I *can* read, Stace," he said, and she stuck her tongue out at him, just as Lili and the girls reached the top of the steps and Tony noticed they were wearing nearly identical, enormous hoodies in different retina-searing colors. With beads. And stuff. Lili in beads? *Claire* in beads? Noticing his gawking, Claire looked down, then back up, blushing.

"Lili bought 'em for us—"

"No, no…it's okay…" Smiling, Tony hugged her to him. "It's just I've never seen you in anything like that before. It looks good on you."

Lili grinned, looked pleased as all hell. "Doesn't it? The color's so pretty with her hair—"

"Mom said we could do cookout tonight," Stacey said to her father.

Rudy squinted up at the nasty sky; a late day storm was quickly bearing down on them. "Not sure about that. But I suppose I could make a fire in the gathering room, we could do hot dogs and roast marshmallows and—" The rest of his sentence was lost in the roar of approval from Daph and the boys. "Then everybody inside," Rudy said, waving them all through the door. He looked back at Tony. "You coming?"

"In a sec," he said, walking back over to the porch steps. A second later he heard rustling bags as Lili settled one hip on the railing.

"Stupid question, I know," she said, "but how are you doing?"

His chest actually ached when he hauled in a lungful of rain-and-pine scented air. "You know, it would help if you weren't so damned nice all the time."

Chuckling, she looked out as the first fat drops began to pounce on the rhododendrons lining the base of the porch. "I could say the same thing," she said quietly. "It would definitely make things easier."

"Dammit, Lil…I didn't expect…I can't…"

"You don't have to explain. In fact, I'd rather you didn't. We both know all the reasons why this can't work. But sometimes, knowing someone cares…" She turned, smiling slightly. "It's lovely, Tony. Truly." She set down the bags to prop her back against a support post, crossing her arms. "But you didn't answer my question."

Tony let his eyes caress hers. "After what you just said? How do you think I'm doing?"

"Sorry. But I wasn't talking about…that. I meant the other."

"Right." Pressing his fingers into the back of his neck, he said. "I called Cole."

Lili's brows shot up. "Already?"

"Yeah. I guess he's been thinking about it and…" He lowered his voice, even though the rain was now pounding the porch roof so hard it was highly unlikely anyone could hear them in the house. "He doesn't want her."

Her head tilted. "Why aren't we sounding happier about that?"

"Because it's not that simple. *Nothing's* that simple," he said on a sigh. "I asked him to put it in writing. He wants me to swear I'll never tell her."

"You can't…" Lili glanced over her shoulder, then whispered, "You can't keep a secret like that forever!"

"Exactly what I said. Bastard hung up on me. So everything's still up in the air." He leaned on his forearms, out far enough to feel a slight spray on his face. "I can just see it now, him showing up out of the blue however many years from now, contrite as all hell and deciding he wants to play dad."

"Surely the law would be on your side, though? If you've been raising her…?"

"You would think. And God knows he'd have a fight on his hands. But that's part of everything I have to sort out." A flash of lightning, then a thunderclap, ripped open the sky. Tony watched the poor rhododendrons cowering in the onslaught, then said, "When are you leaving, exactly?"

He glanced over, saw she wasn't looking at him. "A week from today."

"That soon? Wow."

A smile slid in his direction. "I know, it surprised me, too, when I realized it this morning."

"It'll…be good to get home, right?"

She stretched out one arm, letting the water bounce off her palm. "I suppose," she said, pulling her hand back in and rubbing it on her jeans. "If nothing else, it's time to get serious about sorting out my mother's apartment—" Cutting herself off, she frowned at him. "Do you know I've never lived entirely on my own before?"

"Seriously?"

"Seriously."

"Lookin' forward to that?"

Lili faced front again. "I don't know, to tell you the truth. I always thought I'd like the quiet. The autonomy. Now I'm not so sure. Not that I'm afraid to be by myself, not like my mother was. I just…" Shaking her head, she let the sentence drift off.

Tony cleared his throat. "I—we—should come visit sometime," he said, but she shook her head a second time.

"People always say they'll come visit, but they almost never do." Her eyes swung to his. "I know you're going through hell right now. But you will get through it. You, and the girls. And then you'll go on with your lives and this summer will become another memory." She smiled. "As will I."

His chest seized up. "You sayin' you're never comin' back?"

"Oh, I wouldn't rule it out. But probably not for a long time." She paused. "For obvious reasons."

"I'm sorry, Lil," Tony breathed out.

"For what? For something you can't control? For not being in a position to be what I'd need you to be?"

"Yeah, actually," he said, more pissed about it than he'd expected. "Because you were wrong, the other day, when you said I look at you and just see an older version of the kid I played five million video games with that summer. Believe me, that's not who I'm seeing, Lil. Not who I—"

He jerked away, the rest of the sentence caught in his throat. Thank God she didn't press him to finish it. Instead, she sighed.

"There was a time I used to envy some of my girlfriends, the ones who could fall in love without thinking it to death. It all seemed so easy for them. Until I realized how rarely those relationships stuck." She smiled. "Even a wildflower has to have deep roots to survive. And these gals…so often they looked to the other person to complete them, or they confused love with admiration or infatuation or lust or…" Another sigh. "Or sympathy."

"You feel sorry for me?"

"No," Lili said on a half laugh. "But I am angry for you, which I'm not sure is much better. Angry for the mess you're in, especially angry for what your wife did to you…" She sighed. "I suppose I'm too pragmatic for love to be simple." A pause, then: "And I want to be absolutely sure I'm not confusing it with something else."

"Yeah," Tony said on a breath. "I know what you mean." He rubbed his jaw, then said, "So what now?"

"Now? We go back to Springfield tomorrow and get on with our lives."

"And that's it?"

She smiled at him. "Seems a better alternative to constant frustration, don't you think?"

"Not really, no," he said softly, and she averted her gaze again. "The girls will be with their grandparents again on Saturday, though—"

"And you want me to come clean your bathrooms?"

"Oh, for God's sake, Lili! No, I don't want you to come clean, I want to take you out to dinner! To a real restaurant with tablecloths and candles and everything." Yeah, he had no idea that was coming, either. But as soon as he said it, it made total sense. As much sense as anything made these days, at least. However, judging from her frown, maybe it wasn't making as much sense to her as it did to him.

"W-why?"

"Because I don't want to inflict dry hamburgers on you a second time?"

"No," she said, smiling. "I mean—"

"I know what you mean," Tony said gently, wanting to cup her jaw, to touch that soft skin, to feel her mouth open and warm and giving underneath his again. Still wanting more than he had any right to want. "I just wanna show my appreciation for everything you've done, okay? Just you and me. No kids, no grandparents, no dog. Nobody but us."

Finally, she nodded. "Okay."

"Really?"

"Honestly, Tony...yes. Really."

"You like Italian? Because there's this great little place not far from me, close to the park. We could eat, then go for a walk. Or the other way around, I don't care."

She smiled. "I don't, either. I'll leave it up to you," she said, as a just-awake Josie came barreling outside to graft herself to his legs. Claire stood in the doorway, still in her new hoodie, looking from Tony to Lili, then back.

"You didn't hear her, so I got her up."

"Thanks, honey," he said, flying Josie up into his arms.

"I had a good sleep, Daddy!" the baby said, hugging his neck, and he realized he would kill for her. For all of them. For Lili, too, although he'd keep that to himself.

"Good for you!"

"An' guess what? I went potty, too!"

"No kidding?" he said to Claire.

"No kidding," she said, and they shared a quiet moment of triumph. Every woman in the family had been giving him grief because the kid wasn't potty-trained yet—Susan, especially, had been quite vocal on the subject, insisting she could have Josie out of diapers in a week if Tony would just leave the baby with her—but forcing a kid to use the toilet hadn't been high on Tony's list. He'd figured when she was ready, she'd train. Apparently she was.

Good to know, he thought, looking from Claire to Lili, that somebody was ready for *something*.

* * *

Claire lay awake for a long time, listening to the rain pound the inn's roof and thanking God they were going home tomorrow.

Not that she hated it here or anything—the inn was actually kinda neat and the food was good and it was fun hanging out with Stacey and stuff—but she was *really* tired of feeling like something was going on but nobody would talk about it. Like when they'd been at the falls, and Dad suddenly got that phone call? Don't tell *her* something bad hadn't happened, she could feel it in her bones.

Then there'd been the really strange thing with Lili, after dinner. Since Stacey was, like, texting everybody in the entire universe, Claire'd gotten bored, so she'd gone out onto the porch. The rain had made it darker than usual, except for the light from the gathering room coming through the screen door and windows. So she didn't realize at first Lili was there, too, sitting in the glider at the end of the porch. When the glider squeaked, Claire'd nearly jumped out of her skin.

A second later Claire realized Lili'd been crying, which seemed really weird since she'd been so happy and stuff when they'd gone shopping. Claire hated when grownups cried, because if they weren't in control of things, who was? She meant to go back inside, but instead she heard herself ask Lili if she was okay. Of course Lili said she was fine, trying to make her voice sound normal. But it made Claire uncomfortable and more confused than ever, so she left. Lili came back in a couple minutes after that, but she went up to her room without saying much to anybody—

"Claire? You awake?"

Feeling like she'd gotten an electric shock, Claire rolled over, barely able to see Daphne lying in the other bed, hanging onto the ratty-haired Barbie doll Mom'd given her when she was like two or something. "Yeah, I'm awake."

"C'n I get in bed with you?"

"Sure," Claire said, holding up the covers so Daph could crawl in beside her. The rain had made it so cold, it almost felt like fall. "You have a bad dream or something?"

"Not 'xactly," Daph said, wriggling around until she got comfortable. "I just woke up and felt weird, that's all." Settled, she curled herself around the doll, facing Claire. "And Dad is *seriously* snoring, I can hear him right through the wall."

Claire might've giggled if she hadn't felt so empty inside, sorta like she was hungry except it wasn't food she wanted. She put her arm around her sister and pulled her close, tickly hair and all. "That better?"

"Uh-huh," Daph said with a huge yawn, probably already halfway back to sleep. To tell the truth, having Daph there made Claire feel better, too. She was almost tempted to go get Josie and put her between them, but for one thing the bed wasn't that big, and for another, the rule was once the baby was asleep you did not wake her up unless there was a fire or earthquake or something.

Lightening flashed, followed by a low rumble of thunder. Daph snuggled closer, then whispered, "Today was fun, huh? With Lili?"

"Yeah, I guess," Claire said, although admitting it made her feel bad. Like she was being disloyal to Mom or something. Except Mom wasn't here, for one thing, and the hoodie really was neat—

"Do you think Dad's been acting funny?"

Claire's heart started beating so hard she could hear it in her head. "Don't talk nuts."

"I'm not! Ever since that strange man showed up, it's like he's all the time worried about something."

"You're just imagining stuff." She sneezed, then swiped Daph's hair out of her face. "Go to sleep, everything's fine."

After a few seconds, her sister's breathing slowed down. But Claire's thoughts were running around in her head like that freaked gerbil they had in her second grade classroom that, like, never stopped running on its wheel. Even when it wasn't moving, you'd go to touch it and it would jump and scare you half to death. She felt like that all the time these days, like she never knew when something was gonna jump out at her—

"I think Dad likes Lili," Daphne said, making Claire jump like something *had* popped out at her.

"Jeez, Daph—I thought you were asleep. And of course he *likes* her—"

"I mean *really* like. In fact…" Daph sat up, dragging half the covers with her as she leaned over to looking at the door between Dad's and their room, like she was listening to make sure he was still asleep. Then she snuggled back down and whispered, "I saw Lili and Dad *kissing.*"

Now Claire's skin get cold and sticky, like she was about to throw up. "You're lying."

"Nuh-uh, cross my heart! I came up to get something and the door was open and there they were. And it wasn't a little kiss, either, it was like how he used to kiss Mom."

"That's disgusting, Daphne! Take it back!"

"You can't take something back if it's true!" Daph said, bouncing up a second time and messing up the covers all over again. "I only told you because I thought you'd want to know. Now I'm sorry I did."

With that, she stumbled out of the bed and back to her own, where she yanked her own covers over her shoulders, facing away from Claire. Who was totally confused. If that was true, why had Lili been crying? Of course, maybe she was crying because of something else, maybe…

Claire squeezed shut her eyes, wishing the thoughts just *stop,* already. Then she pushed herself up onto her elbow and whispered, "I'm sorry I got mad. You just surprised me, is all."

After a moment, Daphne flopped back around. "What if Dad asks Lili to marry him, an' she ends up being our new mom—"

"Don't be a bonehead, Daph—Dad would never do that."

She could sorta see her sister's frown in the strange gray light coming through the window. "Why not?"

"Jeez, Daph—she *just* died!"

"She didn't *just* die, that was like before Thanksgiving. And it's not like she's ever c-coming back, is it?" Claire saw her wipe her eyes with the edge of the sheet. "Aren't you tired of feeling sad all the time?"

Claire laid her cheek on her hand. Tired of it? Sometimes she felt like it was going to crush her, it was so heavy. "Sure. But I don't know how to stop it."

"Me neither."

"Really? You don't act like you're sad very much."

"I'm just good at keeping it inside me. Because I hate the way Dad looks when I cry and stuff. But wouldn't it would be nice to feel *really* happy, instead of just pretending?"

Yeah, it sure would. "C'mere," Claire said, moving over so Daph could get in bed with her again. Then she stretched out behind her, whispering, "It's gonna be okay, I promise," over and over until she knew Daph was really asleep, this time.

But Claire stayed awake for a long time after that, now thinking mostly about Lili crying, and how wrong that felt, and Dad kissing her—and how *really* wrong *that* felt—but how, just for a little while, when they'd been shopping, Claire had felt almost okay again. Normal. Not exactly happy, but close enough to remember what it felt like.

And she hated feeling so mixed up, one second just wanting Lili to go away, to go back to Hungary, the next minute not wanting her to leave at all. *I don't want to like you!* she thought, brushing away first one tear, then another, running down her cheeks and tickling her nose as she realized how mad she was at Mom, for dying, for leaving her, for making Dad so sad all the time.

Pulling Daph closer, Claire squeezed shut her eyes, holding in the pain, wondering if she'd ever, ever feel like she used to, before Mom got sick.

Before everything had gotten so stupid and messed up and awful.

Chapter Eleven

By the time they got back to Springfield, of course, Lili had gotten over her little pity fest. The funny thing was, she hadn't even known why she was crying when Claire surprised her out on the porch. Not really. Because she *was* practical. She did know—and accept—that she and Tony weren't meant to be, that her feelings for him were, at the very least, muddied with all sorts of emotions that had nothing to do with love.

Not that she didn't love him. That much she'd admitted to herself long before she'd bought those condoms, still buried underneath a half ton of detritus at the bottom of her bag. But life—and love—wasn't like the romantic comedy films her mother had adored, where little kept the couple apart aside from a few misunderstandings. Clear those up and ta-da! Hearts and flowers. In real life, however, issues happened. Sometimes people were simply on different paths, or the timing sucked, or whatever.

Sometimes—

"Tony's here," Uncle Benny yelled up the stairs.

"I'll be right down!"

Sometimes, she thought as she spritzed on the only one of her aunt's perfumes she actually liked, it really was about seizing the day. Or, in this case—she slipped on her ballerina flats, then reached underneath the loose, gauzy top she'd bought in New Hampshire to readjust her first ever truly sexy bra—seizing the moment.

Although honestly—she felt more like a schoolgirl going out on her first date than a nearly thirty-year-old woman hoping to get lucky.

When she reached the bottom of the stairs, Tony turned from talking to their uncle, his eyebrows lifting, only to immediate crash over his nose.

"What's different?"

Me, Lili thought, then smiled. "Highlights," she said, tossing her hair. "Magda dragged me to her hairdresser yesterday. Said I needed a new look to go with my new life. And no, I'm not going to ask if you like it, because *I* like it so what anybody else thinks is immaterial."

The two men exchanged a look, Uncle Benny shrugging and muttering, "Women, whatchagonna do?" before giving Lili a fond grin. "This one's somethin' else, you know that? Gonna miss her like hell when she goes back."

"Aw…I'm going to miss you, too, Uncle Benny," Lili said, giving him a peck on his whiskery cheek, before Tony opened the door and ushered her outside, his hand on the small of her back sending many, many tingles throughout her entire being.

"So," he said, "walk first? Or eat?"

"Walk, I think," she said. "It's such a lovely evening."

"Yeah. Not too hot."

"No. And a good breeze."

"God," Tony said, laughing softly. "We're talkin' about the weather, for cryin' out loud. Is that pathetic or what? Tell you what—" He took her hand. More tingles. "How about we not talk at all?"

"About anything?" Lili asked, hiking her bag up onto her shoulder.

"Nope, nothing. More than that, how about we pretend, just for the next cuppla hours, like there's nothing else except us, bein' together—" he lifted their linked hands, pointing toward a dense thicket of trees a few blocks down "—going for a walk in the park?"

Lili smiled. "Can you really do that?"

"I sure as hell am gonna try."

So, wordlessly, they walked hand in hand until they reached the expansive park, as lush as anything Lili'd seen in Europe. In the viscous light, thick with humidity and small swarms of gnats, they passed the usual contingent of runners, people walking dogs, parents with kids, until their meanderings eventually took them to the edge of a large, glittering lake, teeming with geese and ducks. Within seconds the water rippled like liquid gold as dozens of the creatures glided toward them begging for a handout, honking like Parisian taxis on the Champs Elysees.

Lili laughed and Tony slipped his arm around her waist, and she leaned into him, savoring his scent, the scene, the bittersweet moment. Then his other arm wrapped around her as well, holding her close, and Lili shut her eyes, loving him, and as if he heard her he gently kissed her temple, making tears crowd her eyes. For a long time they simply stood in each other's arms, afraid to move, to breathe, to break the spell, until a sudden, insistent breeze whipped through the trees, snatching at their hair and clothes. Holding her hair, Lili looked around, noticing that all the leaves had flipped over, baring their gray-green undersides.

Tony looked up. "Holy crap—where'd that come from?" he muttered at the huge, menacing black cloud overhead.

"Come on," he said, grabbing her hand, "my house is closer than Magda's. If we haul ass we just might make it before we get dumped on."

Although Lili was wearing flats, her shorter legs were no match for Tony's as, the thunder taunting them, they sprinted out of the park and through the neighborhood, dodging the first big, fat raindrops. A few blocks from Tony's house the sky burst, instantly drenching them. Blinded, soaked, Lili shrieked with laughter when Tony dragged her through the deluge down the alley behind his house, the garden little more than a battered, soggy blur as they ran across.

Once inside, Tony slammed shut his back door, the rain pummeling against it like thwarted demons. Slicking rain from his eyes with both hands, he shook his head and panted out, "Okay…so maybe…that didn't turn out exactly…the way I saw it in my head."

So wet she was unable to move, Lili started laughing all over again when the dog plodded in, took one look at them and quickly backed out of the room.

"I'll get towels," Tony said, his eyes bouncing up from Lili's chest before he ducked out of the room faster than the dog. Frowning, Lili looked down.

Oh, she thought, blushing so hard her roots hurt.

Stripped to the waist, Tony returned a minute later with the towels to find Lili standing at the sink with her back to him, wringing out the front of that flimsy little top, exposing a whole lot of glistening skin in the process. Tony flexed his hands, mesmerized by a single water drop dangling from the end of a delicate rope of hair that'd worked loose from the helter-skelter knot on top of her head. He watched, barely breathing, as the sparkling drop quivered, then jumped, mating with her neck.

And trickled crookedly down.

At his sucked in breath, Lili jerked around, the mangled shirt hem clutched in her hands. The wet fabric clung to her breasts, her dark nipples clearly visible through her wet bra. Flesh-colored lace, from what he could tell. Not what he would have expected.

But then, nothing about this evening so far had gone according to plan, so…

The aching silence pounded inside his head, elsewhere, as they stood barely five feet apart, the rain battering the windows. Lili swallowed, still fisting the top's hem. Then, clumsily, fiercely, she peeled it over her head and let it drop to the tile floor. Her nipples strained against the bra's flimsy lace, rising and falling with her every breath.

"Lil, you don't—"

"I know," she said, smiling slightly, blushing furiously, as she unhooked the front of the bra with shaking fingers and let it drop, too.

Tony let out a long, pained sigh. "Oh, man…" Then he forced his eyes up to hers, wide and determined and bright with nervousness, and let out another, even more pained sigh. "You sure about this?"

Still trembling, Lili fumbled behind her to brace herself against the edge of the counter. "Okay…I got this far but…could you take over now, please?"

"Lil, sweetheart…I don't have—"

"I do," she whispered, flushing even more. "In my bag." She nodded off to the side. "An assortment. Different sizes, different…kinds. I didn't know what…" She cleared her throat, tried to smile. "What you liked."

What he liked was *nothing,* Marissa had always been on the Pill or used a diaphragm. So it looked like this would be a night of firsts for both of them.

"We never got dinner," he said, inanely, and she let out a short laugh.

"Dinner, I can have when I go back home," she said, her eyes locked in his. "You, I can't."

Slowly, so slowly, Tony approached her, until he was close enough to skim an unsteady finger along her jaw, to capture that strand of wet hair, to gently touch his lips to hers, tasting her trembling, her anticipation.

Tasting his own.

Then he gathered her close, the feel of her nipples against his damp, chilled skin like tiny, hot kisses…the feel of her in his arms making his heart pound. He tucked her head underneath his chin, rocking her slightly. "Why?" he whispered into her wet hair.

She lifted her eyes to his. "Does it matter?"

"Yeah. It does."

Several seconds passed before she said, "I've never regretted any of the choices I've made along the way. But I know if I leave here without finding out what…" Lowering her eyes to his chest, she skimmed her hands down his arms before catching his gaze in hers again. "What it would be like to make love with you, I'll regret *that* for the rest of my life."

Tony paused. "You mean, love as in a figure of speech? Or love as in—"

"What I feel now started a long time ago," she said softly. "Even if I'd convinced myself the seed had died before it fully took root…" She shrugged. "Apparently, it hadn't."

Slowly, Tony lifted his hand, the mix of frustration and need and tenderness practically burning him up inside as he trailed one finger down the cool, still damp skin on her neck, barely…touching, barely moving, watching her breath catch as she once more clutched the counter edge behind her. Without her glasses, her gaze was luminous, curious, a mind-blowing blend of innocence and trust and arousal. Gritting his teeth, ignoring the sweet ache in his groin, he let his finger continue its journey, skimming first one shoulder, then the other…then across her collar bone, dipping his knuckle between her breasts…then across the top of one breast…around the outside…and underneath, gently lifting the soft, warm flesh before gently, so gently, grazing her nipple with his thumb. A funny little sound burbling in her throat, Lili caught herself as her knees buckled. Tony smiled.

"Responsive little thing, aren't you?"

"This is not a s-surprise," she said, biting her lower lip when he gently plucked at the nipple.

Lifting his hands to bracket her jaw, Tony skimmed his thumbs across her cheeks. "Thought you were inexperienced," he whispered, brushing his lips over hers.

"Inexperienced," she said into his mouth. "Not clueless. I know what—" her tongue touched his "—everything does. How it w-works." She reached up to yank the clip out of her hair; it fell over his hands, heavy and wet and smelling of something that turned him on so much he saw stars. "I know my own body, even if no one else does."

Tony realized he didn't have a single thought in his head that wasn't gonna sound stupid the instant it came out of his mouth. And this woman didn't deserve stupid. When he stayed quiet, though, Lili dipped her head to look up at him, the honesty in her eyes nearly doing him in. "Are you worried about breaking my heart?"

"Actually…" On a deep breath, he smoothed his hands down her shoulders. "I'm more worried about you breaking mine. Because I know…" He touched his forehead to hers. "You want honesty? It was gonna be hard enough, letting you go. Letting you go after we have sex…that might kill me. There was nobody before Marissa, okay?" he said to her frown. "Obviously there's been nobody after her. You do the math."

At that, Lili tried to back away. Except pinned against the counter there was nowhere she could go. "Then maybe we shouldn't—"

"Yeah, we should," he said, and she met him halfway in a frantic, openmouthed kiss that nearly blew his skull off, more than making up in enthusiasm what she might have lacked in expertise, her earlier nervousness vanishing like snowflakes on a heated sidewalk.

On autopilot now, Tony hauled Lili up onto the counter, pushing himself between her open legs, which she wrapped obligingly around his hips to pull him in tighter, her breasts pressed against his chest for barely a second before she pushed him away, but only far enough to undo his belt, and he thought, *They sure don't make virgins like they used to.* He palmed one breast, soft and heavy and warm, and angels sang as he seized her mouth in another wild and crazy kiss that went on for a nice little while until she shifted, practically shoving her breast into his mouth—like he needed encouragement—clutching his hair as he tongued and swirled and sucked, harder and harder and harder until she groaned, then gasped, then sighed, a small, sweet sound that broke his heart, that she'd waited so long…waited for him…

Don't be stupid, Tony thought, grazing the taut nipple with his teeth, and she yanked up his head and said, "Take me to bed," and he grinned—a little crookedly, probably—and said, "What, you don't want your first time to be in the kitchen?" and she said, "Not especially, no, although we could put it on the list for later," and Tony moaned, lunged for her bag with its cornucopia of condoms, then wrapped her around him and lifted her off the counter to stagger toward the stairs.

Lili laughed, an unexpectedly throaty sound that seriously threatened his control. "If I put your back out, I'd rather it not be before the fun part of things. I can walk, thank you."

"Not sure I can," Tony muttered, even as he grabbed her hand and hustled up the stairs and into his room, not bothering to shut the door before they crashed onto the bed, kissing like a pair of teenagers and ripping off what was left of each other's clothes. However, through the haze and despite an erection that was soon going to need its own zip code, he realized he couldn't just go for it, that you don't send a rookie out into the big game without at least *some* training.

"What's wrong?" Lili asked when he sat back on his knees, streaking one hand through his hair. "And why aren't you wearing a condom yet?"

"Because you're not ready."

She frowned. "And how would you know this? You haven't even touched me, um, down there." When he frowned, she blew out a sigh. "I told you, I do know how everything works. It's not as if I've never done *anything*. Just not…everything."

Tony cleared his throat. He'd always thought he was pretty easy-going, when it came to talking about sex. So much for that. "So you've, um…"

A blush swept over her collarbone and up her neck. "It's called—"

"I *know* what it's called, for God's sake. What I mean is…" He pushed out a breath. Honestly. "Were batteries involved?"

Her brow puckered for a moment until the light dawned. Then she burst out laughing, looking so damned adorable and sexy and trusting with her hair a mess around her head and her skin all pink and her lips swollen— "No."

"Okay, then." Tony stretched out beside her. "Knees up, honey."

"What are you—? Oh," she said when, smiling, he kissed her, then slipped two fingers inside her. And yes, she was *very* ready. A little stroke there, some pressing there, now for a little stretching…

Lili arched, eyes shut, sucking in a breath, letting it out on a soft, beautiful, "Oooohhhh…."

"You good?" Tony asked, which got a tiny, squeaked, "Mmm-hmm."

He smiled, pulling back, dipping deeper, going where no man—or, apparently, anything else—had gone before. "Let go, Lil," he murmured between kisses. "Let it happen."

"But…but….but—" Oh, man, was she close. "But I want—"

"And you'll get," he murmured, speeding up, shifting to flick his tongue over one tight little nipple. "And it'll be so much better with a little warm-up, trust me…" He tugged and teased and tugged some more, listening for his cues, speeding up and slowing down and speeding up again until—

Yeah, like that.

Then he scooped her close, kissing, gentling, until the tremors subsided. After a moment, Lili looped an arm around him.

"Holy mackerel."

"Somebody's definitely been watching too much American TV. From the freaking *'fifties.* Hey—where ya goin'?"

"Nowhere," she said, sitting up cross-legged with her back to him. As Tony trickled his fingers down her spine, she sighed. "It really is different. As a social activity, I mean." Then she twisted to meet his gaze. "And that was just a *warm-up?*"

Tony grinned. "So it was good?"

"Okay, forget I said that," Lili said, laughing, pretending to escape, laughing even harder when Tony yanked her back down on top of him, threading his hands through her hair and kissing her six ways to Sunday. Then she laid her head on his chest, sighing, and the emotions swamping him…oh, man. And it had nothing to do with her being a virgin or any of that crap. It was just…her. Lili. Lili and him together.

Tony sucked in a deep breath, shutting his eyes. What he'd said before? About how hard it was going to be to give her up?

Yeah. In spades.

He shifted her off him, only to gather her close her again. Pushing her hair out of her eyes, she looked around. "Nice room."

"Marissa did it all herself—" On a groan, Tony shoved his face into the pillow, then gave her *sheepish.* "That was really bad form. Sorry."

That got a tiny smile. And a quick kiss. "I know you shared the room with your wife, Tony. She had very nice taste. We can move on now."

Tony nodded, then said, "So...I gotta ask—this dude you were engaged to? You and he never even fooled around?"

Lili shrugged. "A little, of course. But he—we—never let things get out of hand."

One side of Tony's mouth tucked up. Judging from what he'd just witnessed, how the hell she'd been able to rein herself in this long, he had no idea. "And I still say the man was an idiot."

Lili's fist had been knotted on his breastbone; now her fingers unfurled to toy with the thatch of hair there. "No, I think Peter and I simply weren't right for each other, even though it looked good on paper. He married someone else, a few years ago. I ran into them last year." Propping her chin on her hand, she smiled. "She seemed normal enough. And from everything I could tell, they're quite happy."

"But...?"

"No 'buts.' Not about that, anyway. However, seeing them only confirmed what I'd already realized, that what I thought we had wasn't enough. Wouldn't have been enough, in the long run. I want to be with someone who..." Her lips curved. "Who *can't* say no if I'm saying yes. I want someone who *needs* me. Desperately. Madly." Her gaze speared his. "I want something *real.*"

Tony stilled. "Is this real?"

"Yes," she said simply. "For this moment, it's very, very

real." She hesitated, then reached for a condom, handing it to him.

"Now?" he whispered, taking it from her.

"Now is all we have," she said, lifting her knees.

In the velvety, early evening light, as the rain thrummed overhead and a warm, honeysuckle-scented breeze swirled around them, Lili felt deliciously bombarded. By her emotions, her senses, more acute than she ever remembered before…by a razor-sharp awareness of every atom of her being as Tony guided himself inside her with excruciating care, until, suddenly, there he was, filling her, loving her, and she sighed, thinking nothing had ever felt this good.

Until, that is, he eased out, then pushed back in, and the sweet joy of it brought tears to her eyes.

"You okay?" he whispered, and she laughed and said, "You have no idea, how okay I am," and he brought her legs up to wrap around him and joined them more tightly, deeply, closely still, and something fierce and hungry rose up inside her, making her feel lightheaded, reckless, apart from herself as she tasted his saltiness, then let her head drop back, sucking in a breath when Tony tongued first one hyper-sensitive nipple, then the other, the ache building and building until she thought she'd burst with it.

Then she did, so hard she half wondered if she might die, not much caring if she did or not…until she heard Tony's breathing quicken, and somehow she both relaxed and tensed at the same time, welcoming, absorbing his release.

Afterward, his smile flashed in the near dark, half cocky, half tender, before he softly kissed her forehead, her cheeks, her mouth. "Don't move," he said, carefully withdrawing, and she murmured, "Not a problem." Seconds later they were again a tangle of combined scents and off-sync heartbeats and warm, damp limbs, wrapped in silence and their own thoughts until Tony whispered, "What's goin' through your head?"

Lili laughed softly, even though reality was beginning to creep back in like the moonlight over the windowsill as the clouds, now spent, dispersed. "About how I just lucked out, I suppose." She snuggled closer, kissed his chest. "We could have been terrible together."

"Somehow, I doubt it."

"Not that your ego's overblown or anything."

He chuckled, the sound all rumbly in her ear, then pressed a kiss into her hair. "Sex is a funny thing," he said over the *plonk, plonk* of water dripping from the eaves. "Despite all that crap you read about in magazines or whatever, technique doesn't have nearly as much to do with whether it's good or not as…the other stuff."

"You mean…feelings?"

"Yeah." He paused. "If it's more about being together, bein' close? Then you can have good sex even if it's lousy, if you know what I mean. But if you're just doin' it to do it, then you can hit all the right buttons and still get that 'Is that it?' feeling when you're done. Of course, in an ideal world you can have both, and then it's freakin' fantastic."

Lili paused, then said, "And…?"

"I think that's called fishing, sweetheart," he said on another soft laugh. "But yeah. That was pretty damned good." Another pause preceded, "I could listen to you cry out like that all night."

Toying with his chest hair, Lili said, "You'll have to feed me first."

Silence. "You sure?"

"That I need to eat—?"

"That you wanna spend the night?"

"I'm sure," she said, even as she shooed away the stinging behind her eyes.

* * *

Tony groaned and swore when an obnoxiously cheerful sunbeam stabbed his eyelids the next morning. Batting at both the light and Ed—who'd apparently been waiting patiently for any sign of life—he sat up, at once realizing two things: A) he was naked, and B) the person he'd been naked with was nowhere to be seen. However, both the muted thumping of the dryer in the mudroom and the blissful scent of brewing coffee gave him reason to believe Lili hadn't gone far. Whether she was still naked or not, however, he had no idea.

She wasn't, as it happened, wearing one of his old shirts at she sat at the kitchen table with her chin in her hand and her glasses perched on her cute little nose, engrossed in the Sunday paper, spread out all over the table. Ed trotted over, tail wagging, to nudge her hand; smiling, she leaned over and messed with his soft, floppy ears, talking nonsense to him. Tony's throat clogged at the sight, at how natural and right it seemed, her sitting there at his table, wearing his shirt, talking stupid to the dog. Just as natural and right as falling asleep with her tucked against his chest after a night of playing catch-up.

"I'm surprised you can move," he said from the doorway, startling her. And that was before she realized he hadn't bothered to put anything on. God, he loved when she blushed.

"I can't, actually," she said when she recovered. Eventually her eyes moved up to his face. "Which is why *you* get to do breakfast."

Smiling, Tony ambled over to give her a kiss. "Not a problem." And another. "So why don't you go take a hot bath while I rustle up some toast or something?"

"Good idea." She braced her hands on the table and pushed herself upright. "I put our wet things in the dryer, by the way, so I'll have something to wear when…um, later."

Their gazes caught. "This is totally up to you," Tony said, "but the kids don't come back until tonight. The rest of the day is ours."

She paused, her eyes twinkling. "You think we should go to church?"

"And get struck by lightning? I think not."

Laughing, she stood on tiptoe to kiss him, then sort of hobbled away.

As Tony poured himself a cup of coffee, he heard the water thunder into the bathtub upstairs. Whining, the dog dropped a disgusting tennis ball at Tony's feet, then backed away, daring him to grab it as the dryer buzzed. "Forget it," he muttered, going to pull out their clothes. Boxers were dry, jeans weren't. Whatever. He put them on, barely getting the jeans zipped when the dog went bonkers out in the entryway.

"Shut up, ya stupid mutt!" Tony yelled, figuring it was somebody walking another dog or kids on bikes or a leaf falling off a tree. But no, he realized as his front door flew open and Daphne barreled into the house, followed by her sisters and grandparents.

What this was, was a catastrophe.

Chapter Twelve

"What are you guys doing home?" Tony asked as his precious time alone with Lili vaporized right in front of his eyes. And thanking *God* the dryer had buzzed when it had, otherwise he'd be flashing his in-laws.

"Claire and the baby both caught colds," Susan said, handing Josie to Tony with a brief frown at his bare chest. Thumb in mouth, the baby curled into him, sniffling. Tony strained to hear upstairs—no water running, no singing, no telltale footsteps. With any luck he could at least get rid of Susan and Lou before Lili was finished with her bath. How he'd explain her to the kids, however…

He looked at Claire, the picture of misery with the splotchy face, puffy eyes, the works, and Daddy mode kicked in.

"You don't feel good, baby?"

"Not really," she said in a scratchy voice as Josie—who'd never let a thing like a runny nose actually stop her—wriggled to get down. "Move, dog!" she said, her voice more gravelly than usual as she shoved the overjoyed mutt out of her path on her way to the kitchen.

"We would've gladly kept 'em," Lou said, hands in pockets, "but Claire said she wanted to come home." He gave Tony a meaningful look. "So we didn't push it."

"Come on, Nana," Daph said, waving her grandmother toward the kitchen. "I'll show you were we keep all the cooking stuff—"

"Cooking stuff?" Tony said, thinking, *Oh, hell no.*

"Yes, I told the girls I'd make pancakes here—"

"*No!* I mean," he said at Susan's frown, "I haven't been to the store yet this week, I don't have any mix or anything—"

"That's perfectly all right, dear," Susan said, gliding past him toward the kitchen, hauling a bulging tote bag. "I brought everything we need. It's just not Sunday without pancakes," she said, nearly tripping over the baby when she suddenly popped back out into the hallway...shuffling merrily along in Lili's shoes.

Okay, no need to panic, Tony thought, panicking, *maybe nobody will notice, maybe I can somehow get Lili's clothes to her and she could just slip away—*

Tony herded everybody toward the kitchen, figuring there'd be so many people nobody would notice if he disappeared for a couple of minutes, only to spot Lili's bag on the counter.

About the same time Claire did.

She turned, accusation sharp behind puffy lids. "Why's Lili's bag here?" she asked, just as Lili herself appeared in the kitchen doorway, hair dripping wet, wrapped in a towel, gingerly dancing only to music she could hear through the tiny plug in her ear from Tony's MP3 player which he'd left on the bathroom sink. All heads turned in her direction the same instant she realized they weren't alone.

"Lili!" Josie squealed, shuffling toward her with her arms outstretched. "I gots your shoes—!"

"Oh, dear God," Lili whispered, blushing furiously. "I'm so sorry, I…" She vanished, as, behind him, Susan muttered a soft, "Oh, Tony," and Claire yelled, "You *said* nothing was going on! Both of you! You *promised*—!"

"*Enough!* All of you!" Tony bellowed, earning him a roomful of shocked expressions. He stormed to the mudroom and snatched Lili's clothes off the top of the dryer, then strode back through the kitchen, pausing only long enough to grab Lili's bag and lift Josie out of her shoes, adding them to the pile.

"I'm sure everybody's got plenty to say," he said, backing out of the room, "but I'm afraid it'll hafta wait for a few minutes. Try not to talk *too* badly about me while I'm gone."

Claire's wails followed him as he took the stairs two at a time to find Lili in his bedroom, sitting on the edge of the bed, clutching the damp towel to her breasts and staring at nothing in particular. As Tony shut the door behind him, she shook her head and whispered, "That was the most mortifying moment of my life. I never meant…"

"I know, I know," Tony said, sitting beside her and swinging an arm around her cool, bare shoulders. It was like hugging a statue. "It'll be okay, honey, I swear—"

"I'm not deaf, Tony. I can hear Claire from here, even through the closed door. From her standpoint, I did exactly what I told myself—what I told *her*—I'd never do. And the look on your mother-in-law's face—"

"We just caught 'em off guard—"

"Then you really don't understand just how deep something like this goes." She grabbed the clothes out of his hand, dumped the towel and unceremoniously stepped into her panties, then clumsily put on her bra. "Last night," she said, jerking up her skirt and fumbling with the back zipper, "was a dream. *This* is reality. Your reality, at least. Claire would never accept me as a replacement for her mother. And your in-laws…" Grabbing her blouse from the bed, she shook her head.

"And none of that matters because you're leaving anyway, right? Because—how did you put that?—what you feel is all mixed up with a bunch of other stuff?"

Lili's eyes darted to Tony's, her trembling hands stilling on the crumbled top's pearl buttons. They watched each other in brittle silence for several seconds before she rammed her feet into her shoes and grabbed her bag from where he'd dumped it on the dresser. When she reached the bedroom door, however, she turned and said quietly, "Face it, Tony...I—*this*—was an interlude. Which we both knew, so no hard feelings. But boy," she said, her eyes watering, "if there was *any* doubt that I don't belong here, in this house...in your life..."

She shook her head, then slipped from the room and ran down the stairs. Moments later the front door slammed. Tony didn't move, Lili's words echoing in his head. Eventually, however, his breathing returned to something resembling normal and he went back downstairs, only to have Lou waylay him in the hallway.

"We need to talk, Tone."

"I should really see to Claire—"

"She can wait," his father-in-law said, taking him by the arm and steering him out front. "Susan's got things under control for the next little while."

Outside, Tony sank onto one of the wicker chairs on the porch, leaning forward with his hands clamped together and staring toward the street. "Obviously Lili and I never meant for anybody to find out," he said. "Or to hurt anybody—"

"You including yourself in that equation?"

He frowned up at the older man as anger bellowed inside him, drowning out the hundred other emotions all screaming for attention. "Twenty-four lousy hours to ourselves," he bit out. "*For* ourselves. Was that so much to ask?"

Finally, Lou sat in the nearby matching loveseat, his fingers laced over his potbelly. "Is it serious?"

Tony snorted. "Would it matter if it was?" He blew out a sharp breath. "When you're eighteen it's all about you. Parents, other people…their opinions mean squat. Then you grow up, have some kids of your own, and it's never just about you anymore. It can't be, if you're a decent parent." When Lou remained silent, Tony's gaze slid back to his. "Why aren't you sayin' anything?"

The other man pushed himself back up, his hands rammed into his chinos' pockets as he crossed to a straggly pot of moss roses that had pretty much been left to their own devices. "Believe it or not, Susan and I really are concerned about you, that this…thing is a whaddyacallit. A rebound. A way to deal with the shock."

"It's been nearly ten months, Lou—"

"I'm not talkin' about Marissa's passing," Lou said quietly, turning, and for the first time Tony saw an anguish of an entirely different kind in his father-in-law's eyes. Tony's stomach plummeted.

"Holy hell…you knew?"

"Yeah."

"When—?"

"Rissa broke down, confessed to her mother not long after she found out she was sick. Susan begged her to tell you the truth then, but she said she couldn't, that she'd take care of it in her own time." He paused. "So about a month ago, we get this note through your guys' lawyer. All it said was, 'By the time you get this, Tony will know.' Susan and me, we kept waitin' for you to say somethin'—"

"Yeah. Like I could've done that." At Lou's slight smile, Tony took a deep breath. "How much did she tell you?"

"That she had an affair, although she didn't mention names." He scratched behind his ear. "That she wasn't sure the baby was yours."

"She's not," Tony said quietly, and Lou swore. Which he

did again after Tony explained everything that had transpired on that front.

"She cheated on you with the Jamison kid?"

"He's not a kid anymore, Lou."

"Whatever. Thought he was a sleazeball then, now I know why. Look, you need any legal help—about keeping the baby, I mean—I know more'n one pitbull lawyer. Don't worry about the money, we'll foot the bill. Anything to make sure you keep Josie." Lou blinked, clearing his throat. "I don't know why the hell Rissa did what she did. I do know she was sorry for it, said it wasn't your fault, that you'd been a good husband. I also know if she said it once, she said it a million times, what a good father you were. Are. If we overstepped— about wantin' to take the girls off your hands, I mean—I apologize. We were just tryin' to help, but…" He shrugged.

Knowing what it took for Lou to say all of that, Tony smiled. "Thanks, I appreciate it. All of it. But God willing we won't have to sic any of your lawyer buddies on the guy…" Tony cupped his mouth, his eyes burning.

"Dammit, Tone—you don't deserve to be goin' through this crap," Lou said gently, then sighed. "And Susan and me, we wanna see you happy. See you married again someday. But now…" He shook his head. "Look, it's not hard to guess what you've been going through the past few weeks. That you're probably not thinking real straight. I mean, gettin' news like that—who would, right?" Lou rubbed his mouth. "Not the best time to start a relationship, that's all I'm saying."

"I know that," Tony said softly. Aching. Once again trying to make sense of something that didn't. "So did Lili. It wasn't… There weren't any expectations on either side, okay? She's leaving in a few days, anyway. So that's…that."

"It's for the best, Tone. Believe me. Because you've got a lot on your plate right now. And you're gonna have even more when you tell Claire and Daphne about…that Josie's only their half sister."

Tony's head jerked up. "The kid's *ten,* Lou. And nowhere near over her mother's death. Why on earth would I dump even more crap on her?"

"I'm not saying you hafta to go into any great detail or anything. But it's gonna come out, probably sooner rather than later. And I'm just guessing here, but if Claire doesn't hear it from you, there's gonna be hell to pay down the road when she does find out."

"No argument there. But she's my kid. And it's up to me to break the news to her. When it feels right."

"Yeah, yeah, of course. Totally your call. But Claire's a sensitive kid, she already knows something's up. She even said as much to her grandmother. So you might wanna think about heading things off at the pass. Just sayin'."

The soft whine of the screen door brought Tony's head around. His mother-in-law, twisting her wedding ring, worry in her eyes. Which Tony saw flick to Lou, silently asking the Big Question, no doubt. About Josie. Saw, too, the older man's slow head shake. He'd witnessed that telepathic communication thing between couples before, although rarely in his own marriage. Lili and he, however—

"Where're the girls?" he asked, turning away from Susan's wretched expression. His own, even more wretched, thoughts.

"Daph and Josie are out back with the dog, Claire's up in her room." She came up to him to wrap one arm around his shoulders, bending over to give him a brief hug. "I'm so sorry, honey. About…about all of it." She paused, then said softly, "Claire's pretty upset—you should probably go talk to her."

Tony stood, looking his mother-in-law in the eye. "Yeah, well, she's not the only one," he said, then banged back the screen door and went inside to go upstairs, desperately wanting to do the right thing by everybody and having no earthly idea how to do that. Hell, at this point he didn't even know what the "right" thing *was* anymore.

Claire was lying on her side on top of her covers, hugging Clifford The Big Red Dog and suddenly looking impossibly small. Tony sat beside her, palming her forehead.

"It's okay," she said, "I don't have a fever. I just feel like crap."

He let it slide. "You eat any breakfast?" She shook her head, not looking at him. No surprise there. On both counts. "Wanna talk?" he asked gently, stroking her hair away from her face. Another head shake.

Seeing her so tiny and vulnerable and tender beside him, he knew no way could she deal with the stuff about her mother and Josie. Not today, at least. Even so, he knew Lou was right, that the longer Tony put this off, the harder it was gonna be. On everybody. God knew acting like nothing was wrong sure hadn't done his marriage any favors, he thought as this brutal sense of loss roared through him—of his wife, in more ways than one; the threat of losing Josie, despite Lou's legal connections; the horrible, gaping hole in his chest when Lili walked out of his room earlier.

That he might somehow lose Claire, too, through his own idiocy—

"C'n I ask you something?" she asked.

"Sure. Anything."

She rolled over, her eyes slightly unfocused without her glasses. "And you *swear* to tell me the truth? Cross your heart?"

"Yeah," Tony said, crossing that heart, banging like hell in his chest. "I swear."

"Why was Lili here?"

Tony took a deep breath. "Because she spent the night."

"Like a sleepover?"

"Sorta."

"Did she sleep in your bed?" When Tony hesitated, Claire let out a sigh of her own. "My friend Jocelyn at school? She told me how her mom sometimes lets her boyfriend sleep over."

"Often?" Tony said, horrified despite himself.

"I don't know, she didn't say. Well?"

"Yeah, baby. She did. But you weren't—"

"Supposed to find out?"

"No, actually." When she made a face, Tony said, "The last thing either of us wanted to do was upset you, baby, I swear—"

"So she's your girlfriend?"

Uh, boy. "Lili's going back to Hungary, cupcake. So it doesn't matter."

Claire sat silently for several seconds, her brow knotted, before she climbed off the bed and went to her dresser to get something out of the top drawer. When she turned, clutching the crumpled piece of paper, Tony felt like he'd been struck by lightning.

"Where...when did you find that?"

"A couple of days ago. Daph'd used up all my pencils, so I went to your office to look for some. I found this in the drawer. I would've put it back, but I was afraid Daph might find it...she p-practically reads better than m-me now..."

"Oh, God, baby...come here." Once he had her safe in his arms, he set Marissa's letter on the bed beside them, then asked, "Why on earth didn't you say something then?"

"It was right before Nana and Gramps c-came to pick us up, there wasn't time." She pulled away, tears crested on her lower lashes. "Is it true?"

After a moment, Tony nodded. "Yeah, honey. It's true."

"Even the part about Josie?"

"That, too."

She threw herself back into Tony's arms, the tears coming

fast and furious now. "Wh-why? Why would Mom d-do that?"

"I guess we'll never know, baby," Tony said, rubbing between her shoulder blades and feeling like he was being ripped apart.

He had no idea how long he held her, letting her cry her eyes out, until she said, in a tiny, shaky voice, "I just wish everything would stop f-feeling like a roller coaster you can't get off of."

In silent agreement, Tony pulled her closer.

"Vat are you doing?" Magda asked from Lili's doorway.

"Packing," she said, shoving a half dozen folded tops into her largest traveling bag, splayed on top of Mia's old bed.

"But your flight isn't for three days yet."

"I'm on standby for an earlier one."

Magda *smack-smack-smacked* across the carpet, clamped her hands on Lili's arms and swung her around. "Vat happened?"

"Nothing," Lili said, on the verge of exploding from trying to hold in her emotions. "I'm just ready to go home, that's all."

"And I don't suppose zis hes anysing to do vis you staying out all night?"

"N-no."

Magda sighed, pushed Lili down onto the pale pink chenille bedspread, ball fringe and all, then sat in the rose-patterned chair across from her, her hands folded on her lap. "I hed hoped you vould hef better sense zen that," she said, not unkindly.

"Yeah, well," Lili said, realizing how much Tony had influenced her speech, "you were the one who said Tony needed me."

"Not exactly vhat I hed in mind," her aunt said, then sighed. "Do you love him?"

Lili nodded.

"So...vas last night worth ze heartache?"

In spite of everything, Lili smiled. "Not that I have a lot to compare it with...but yes. It was."

Eyebrows lifted. "Don't tell me zat vas your first time?"

"Then I won't tell you."

Magda crossed herself, muttering in Hungarian, then squinted at her.

"Yes," Lili said wearily, "we used protection, don't worry." The squint didn't let up. The squint, apparently, was a living thing. "It's not meant to be, okay? There's far too much going on in Tony's life right now...and the girls—well, Claire, anyway—aren't ready...and anyway, I'm supposed to be figuring out what my purpose is in life, and—"

"And zis is all BS and you know it."

"What it is," Lili said softly, getting up to continue her packing, "is a case of the pieces not fitting. I can't wedge myself into his life, Magda," she said when her aunt snorted. "And damned if I'm going to do to Claire what Mama did to me."

Her aunt gave her a look both sympathetic and curious before she sighed again. "I told Sonja she was making a huge mistake—"

"It's okay, we worked through all of that. Eventually. But I refuse to be the bad guy between Tony and *his* daughter."

"And you can spare me ze melodrama, okay?"

"I'm not being melodramatic. I'm being...practical," Lili said, tucking a pair of jeans into the bag.

"Vat you're being," Magda said, slamming her palms against her thighs before she stood, "is a big, fat coward, running avay instead of taking five minutes to see if maybe zere's a solution you heffen't thought of." When Lili frowned at her, she huffed. "You think zere veren't issues ven I fell in love vis Benny? Zat my family didn't hef a cow ven I said I vas leaving ze circus, leaving behind everyzing I efer knew to marry some stranger? But my heart," she said, pressing her bosom, "told me to take zat risk. Marrying somebody ven your heart is broken, like your mother…" Her lips pressed together, she shook her head. "But if your heart is whole, zat is somesing else entirely."

Lili zipped her bag closed, then hauled it off the bed to set it on the floor. "And what makes you think *Tony's* heart is whole?" she said softly, turning to her aunt.

Who, amazingly, had nothing to say to that.

Chapter Thirteen

Tony nearly jumped out of his skin when he rolled over in bed to find JoJo and Ed staring at him. In rapid succession, Tony glanced at the clock—holy crap, it was nearly nine!—bolted upright, shoved the dog out of his face and pulled Josie onto the bed. She was dressed in shorts and a little top and her hair looked like it'd been combed. Sorta. Ed crawled up, too, to burrow under the sheet, leaving his butt on Tony's pillow. Nice.

"How long've you been up?" he said to Josie.

"Since morning," she said, shrugging. "Claire got me. We had f'osted f'akes." She patted his face, only to jerk her hand back, frowning. "Ick. You gots pokies."

Probably because he hadn't shaved in two days. Might not, either, for the rest of the summer. As rebellions went, it was kinda lame. But a guy can only work with what he's got.

The baby molded herself to his bare chest, well underneath the pokies, as Tony rubbed his gritty eyes. Wasn't until after two before he'd finally talked Claire down off the ledge, five before he finally fell asleep himself. Then it was one rotten dream after another, over and over, a continuous loop of anger and worry and anxiety and regret—

A poor James Brown impersonation came in through the open window. Hauling Josie onto his hip, Tony climbed out of bed and padded over to the window in his boxers to see Hollis and Daphne already out in the garden, doing…stuff.

"Hi, Hollis!" Josie called, which of course brought the kid's grinning face up to look at the window.

"Hey, there, pretty baby." He winced. "And not so pretty daddy. Your five o'clock shadow lose track of time or what?"

"Shut up," Tony grumbled, then looked at Josie, regarding him curiously. "Don't say that. Ever."

"'Kay," she whispered, all that trust in her eyes, and he reminded himself for the thousandth time, that the kids came first. That he had his priorities straight, dammit. That it didn't matter that he already missed Lili with an intensity that went way beyond painful—

"Came over to see how the garden did with the storm, but I see it came through just fine. 'Cept you probably should've brought those tomatoes in."

"Thought about that," Tony said, although of course veggie rescue missions hadn't even been a blip on the old radar that evening, a thought which only made him grouchier than he already was. "Then I decided since I'll be eighty before we use up the tomatoes we already picked, it wasn't worth the bother."

"Good point," Hollis said, adding, "I went ahead and put on coffee," and Tony's mood lifted a little.

A half hour later, beard banished, caffeine mainlined and Josie happily watching Elmo and his little furry friends, Tony and Ed wandered out onto the back porch, Tony toting his second cup of coffee as well as a glass of orange juice for

Hollis, who didn't do "that hard stuff." As the kid righted storm-battered tomato cages, Daphne the Mud Puppy happily yanked weeds on the other side of the garden. Hollis threw him a grin.

"Gardening really ain't your thing, is it, Mr. V.?"

"What was your first clue?"

Straightening, the kid moseyed over to the porch and sank onto the bottom step, taking the glass from Tony. "Daphne said Lili was here yesterday morning." He took a sip of the juice. "Wearin' a towel."

"Brat," Tony muttered, and Hollis chuckled.

"So, you two…?"

"No. I mean…" Tony pushed out a sigh. "She's leaving in a couple of days."

"You don't sound too happy about that."

Tony grunted.

"So you just lettin' her go? Man," he said, wagging his head, "talk about *dumb*."

"Hollis. Stop. It's complicated."

"No, it's not. You love the woman, you do whatchu gotta do to keep her, you hear what I'm sayin'? You been through a whole lotta crap this last little while, Mr. V., doncha think it's time you grab a little happiness for yourself?"

"It doesn't work that way. And who says I love her?"

"That look on your face right now, for one thing. What? You think it's too soon? That people might talk smack about you because you're not honorin' your wife or something?"

"It had occurred to me."

"Hell, Mr. V.—it's not like you cheatin' on the woman. She dead. She not comin' back. And you know how you were always on us to grab opportunities, to not let 'em slip through our fingers? Seems to me maybe you should take your own advice." He got up, handing Tony the empty glass. "I gotta go, signing up today for some classes today at the community college." He extended one hand for Tony to slap and grab, then sauntered off around the side of the house.

While Tony was irritably musing about how straightforward everything seemed when you were eighteen, Claire appeared at the back door. Frowning. Although her cold was better today, her outlook on life was not. Tony couldn't say as he blamed her.

"Mailman says you gotta sign for something."

With a weary sigh, Tony got up, handed her the empty glass and dragged himself through the house to the front door, frowning at the large brown envelope the carrier held hostage until Tony signed the little green card and handed it back. He'd barely shut the front door before he ripped it open, scanning the very legal-looking papers with the notary's seal on the bottom. And the handwritten letter accompanying them.

"Holy crap," he whispered when the important parts sank in, the relief that rushed over him so strong it knocked the wind right out of him. He dropped to the bench to read the affidavit a second time, savoring every word. By the third read-through the words on the page began to dance around the thousands of other words in his head—Lili's and Claire's and Hollis's and Lou's, all those words from all those people who either had a stake in or opinion about what Tony should or shouldn't do with his life…and when he should or shouldn't do it. And through all those thousands of words, he only heard—

"Dad? What is it?"

Not those.

But when he looked up and saw Claire standing in the living room archway, Josie in her arms, and another wave of relief surged through him as he grinned at his baby—*his* baby, who nobody could ever take away from him, not now, not ever—a thought slammed him right between the eyes:

That he could no more let Lili, and what they had together, go without a fight than he could Josie, or Claire, or Daph.

That this wasn't an either/or thing. That—and here was the kicker—this wasn't really only about *his* happiness.

"We have to talk, sweetheart," he said, patting the bench beside him.

"Yeah. I know," she said, startling him, before saying to Josie, "How about you watch one of your movies?" before carting her away, saying to Tony over her shoulder, "I'll be right back."

Wait. What?

Sorry, Mom, I know you hated us watching too much TV, but this is an emergency, Claire thought as she set JoJo in front of the flat screen television with one of her Elmo DVDs. Although between her stuffy nose and all the stuff about Mom—she and Dad had talked for like *hours* last night—she hadn't slept much. But weirdly, when she woke up? Her head felt completely clear. About some things, anyway. Like about how, even though Claire still didn't understand why Mom had done what she had, and it hurt, that couldn't ruin the good memories, or change how Claire felt about her. Not if she didn't let it.

And that—if she was being really, really truthful—the only times she hadn't felt like total crap the past few weeks had been when Lili'd been around.

And she was guessing if you asked Dad? He'd say he felt pretty much the same way.

Claire walked back out to the entryway, her arms crossed over her new hoodie. Dad smiled. "A little warm for that, isn't it?"

"I'm fine," she said, shrugging. "So. What was in the envelope?"

"Excellent news," Dad said, smiling bigger than she'd seen in a long, long time. "We don't have to worry about giving Josie up." He waved the papers. "Ever."

Claire felt her eyes go all buggy. "Really?"

"Really. But…" He leaned forward, looking right into her eyes. "When I realized how good I felt about knowing I was never gonna lose Josie," he said in this real quiet voice, "I realized something else. And I know you might not like it, and God knows your grandparents are gonna have a fit but—"

"But you don't want Lili to leave."

She'd never seen that look on Dad's face before, like he was so shocked he didn't know what to say. Then he held out one arm, waving Claire over to sit on his lap. "It's killin' me, the thought of her leaving," he said, all soft and stuff, then touched his forehead to hers. "Just like it would've killed me to lose Josie. Like it would to lose any of you guys. I love her, baby," he said, giving her a squeeze. "Not more than you or your sisters, not more than Mom, but…just as much."

Okay, just say it— "I don't want Lili to leave, either."

Dad looked at her really hard. "Not exactly the vibes you were giving off yesterday."

"I know, I…" Claire pinched her mouth together, then pushed out, "When I saw Lili standing there in the towel, it really freaked me out…" She looked up at Dad. "I got scared."

Dad hugged her shoulder. "Yeah. I know. But now you've changed your mind?"

Claire frowned so hard it hurt. "It's more…I think I figured out which were the good thoughts and which one's weren't. And I decided to go with the good thoughts."

"Sounds like a plan," Dad said.

After a moment, she said, "Does Lili love you, too?"

"I think so."

"So…if you asked her to marry you and stuff, she'd say yes?"

Dad got a funny look on his face. "That, I don't know."

"What do you mean, you don't know? If you love each other—"

"Loving somebody doesn't mean everything automatically falls neatly into place," Dad said, then let out a big breath. "Or that you can't get hurt down the road."

"You mean…like what happened with Mom?"

He nodded, then said, "But Lili and Mom are very different people, with different ways of looking at things, so…"

When Dad didn't finish his sentence, Claire figured that meant he didn't want to say anything bad about Mom, but she got it, anyway—that he didn't think Lili would ever do what Mom did. Claire didn't know why, but somehow she didn't think she would, either. Because Lili and Dad together felt way different than Mom and Dad had. It wasn't a happy thought, but it was an honest one.

Looking down at her hands on top of Dad's, Claire said, "One day, before Mom got sick, I found her crying. She wouldn't tell me why. But she said…" Claire felt her jaw wobble. "She said not to tell you, it would only make you unhappy." Her eyes burning, she looked at Dad. "Do you think she was crying because of what she did?"

Dad pulled her into his arms and laid his cheek on her head. "Maybe. I think she felt really, really bad about it."

Claire leaned into him, liking how he smelled, like soap and the stuff he used after he shaved. It made her feel safe. Sort of. Because then she sighed and said, "It's so scary, letting yourself love somebody."

She felt Dad's quiet laugh in her hair. "Ain't that the truth?"

Sitting up, she pushed her glasses up on her nose. "If…if Lili…" She frowned, not even sure what she was asking. "This would mean a *lot* of changes, huh?"

"Oh, yeah," Dad said. "Lots." He bent his head slightly to look into her eyes. "Could you deal with that?"

Claire thought for a moment, then shrugged. "It's sure worth a shot."

Dad laughed, then held her tight again for a long time, not saying a word.

Of course, Tony's first impulse—with Daphne's shrieked encouragement—was to go straight over to Lili's and make a complete idiot of himself. But it seemed only right that he make an idiot of himself with Lou and Susan first. So he shooed the girls upstairs, hauled in a breath, and hit number "1" on the old speed dial.

"Tony," Susan said when she answered, "what—"

"Could you put Lou on, too? I got something to tell you. A couple of somethings, actually."

Took a few seconds to get the whole conference call thing worked out, but once everybody was connected Tony told them about Josie, including a lot of stuff he hadn't told Claire—that Cole had apparently come clean to his wife and set up a money market account in Josie's name. That while he'd be willing to get to know her someday, if Josie wished it, he saw no reason to disrupt anyone's lives more than they'd already been. That he left it up to Tony, whenever he felt the time was right to tell Josie the truth.

When the relieved congrats died down, he said, "And now for the hard part."

"What hard part, dear—?"

"Suze, for godssake, let the boy talk. What is it, Tone?"

Deep breath. "You know, we have so little control over what happens in our lives, no idea when somebody's gonna come into it that…" He rubbed a hand over his face. "Okay, cut to the chase—I'm sorry, you guys, but I can't just let Lili walk out of my life. I thought I could, I thought it was the right thing to do, but…it isn't. At all."

Silence. Finally, Lou spoke.

"But…Claire…?"

"Totally on board. They all are." Tony paused. "The girls love Lili. As much as I do. And when I see what she's done for Claire…I know it's…what's that word?"

"Precipitous?" Susan put in.

"Yeah. That. And I don't even know if this is a definite thing, if *she's* ready for this. For us. But I've spent far too much time recently feeling bad about stuff that wasn't my fault. And Lili's the only person with the guts to not let me get away with that crap. How can I walk away from somebody like that? So I gotta find out, if there's a chance. Not just for me, for the girls, too."

"Oh, Tony," Susan started, but Lou said, "Are you even listening to the boy, Susie?"

"But—"

"Here's a news flash, sweetheart," Lou said gently, "this isn't about us. But, Tone—are you absolutely sure?"

God knows Tony couldn't tell them the seed for what he felt now had lain dormant for nearly fifteen years. And if Marissa hadn't died, if they'd been able to fix their marriage, it would have never blossomed. He knew that as well as he knew his own name. But not going after something because of what might have been made no sense whatsoever.

"You know I loved Rissa with everything I had in me," he said quietly. "I feel exactly the same way about Lili. And believe me, I'm thinking straighter than I ever have in my life. This isn't a rebound, Lou, or about me being lonely or whatever. It's…." He heard Lili's voice in his head. "It's real."

He heard muffled conversation for a few minutes before Lou came back on the line. "Then I suppose we got no choice but to trust you're gonna make the right decision."

"Thanks," Tony said, trying not to tear up. "I really do love you guys—"

"Oh, for God's sake—get the hell off the phone and go get the girl!"

Grinning, Tony went back inside. "Anyone up for goin' over to Aunt Magda's?" he called out, and assorted little girls thundered down the stairs.

"*Please* tell me we're not walking," Claire said, shoving Josie's sandals onto her feet.

"Like I'm gonna take twenty minutes to get there instead of a minute and a half? No way."

But when Magda answered her front door shortly after-wards, jumping back in slight alarm when Daph, Claire and Tony all yelled "Is Lili here?" she pressed a hand to her chest and let out a small, distressed cry.

"No, she's not—Benny took her to ze airport an hour ago!"

"What time does her plane leave?" Claire said, worried.

"Magda said two-thirty."

"But it's already—"

"I know what time it is, baby," Tony said, veering around cars on I-91 like he was playing Grand Theft Auto. Keeping one eye on the road with *all those stupid cars in his way, dammit,* he spared her a quick smile. "It's okay, we're gonna make it."

"You swear?"

"On my life," he said through gritted teeth, zooming down the road leading to airport parking. "Okay, here's the plan— we park, I get the baby, Daph takes Claire's hand, Claire takes mine, then nobody lets go of anybody until I say so. Got it?"

"Got it," both girls chimed beside and behind him, Josie echoing her own a soft "Got it," a second later.

Then they were running through the terminal like a pos-sessed, lopsided bug, Daphne and Josie laughing, Claire panting, until Tony came to a screeching halt in front of an Arrival/Departure screen, whipping the other two around him.

"Has her plane left yet?"

"No," Tony said, heart in throat. "But it's boarding. Come *on!*"

And they were off again, only to come to another screeching halt in front of the squat, tough-looking security gal checking boarding passes.

She held out her hand, bored.

"We're not passengers, we're trying to reach someone about to leave on the British Airways flight to Amster—"

"Then you can't go past this point, sorry." Looking around them, she motioned for the next passenger.

"You don't understand, her cell's apparently dead, I don't have any way of getting hold of her and this is important—"

"No, *you* don't understand that I cannot let you through without a ticket or special permission from the airlines." She checked the man's printout and waved him through to screening. "British Airways' counter is right over there. Next! Keep it moving—"

"The plane's freaking boarding, lady! If I don't get to her—"

"And if you don't stop impeding these people with actual tickets trying to make their flights, I'ma hafta take action, mister...*what?*" she said with an irritated huff when Claire tugged on her sleeve.

"I'm sorry my Dad's acting crazy, but see, our mom died last year? And none of us thought we'd ever want somebody else to be our mother? Or in Dad's case, his wife? Only then Lili—she's the lady we're trying to keep from getting on her plane?—came to visit and, well, we all fell in love with her." She shrugged as Tony watched, stunned. "Especially our Dad. And if we don't get to her before she gets on the plane, she'll go back to Hungary and we'll never see her again."

The woman's eyes shot to Tony's. "You put the child up to this?"

"No. Swear to God—"

"Daddy!" Daph shrieked, blasting his eardrums. "Look! Way down there!"

Everybody—and he meant everybody, passengers, security personnel, the works—turned to look where Daphne pointed. And there, trudging up from the gates, dragging a suitcase the size of Rhode Island behind her, her hair a bedraggled mess and her glasses crooked, was Lili.

His Lili.

Okay, he hoped *his* Lili. Nothing in writing yet.

"That her?" the security lady said, and Tony's heart burst in his chest.

"Yeah," he said as the kids started screaming "Lili! Lili!" at the tops of their lungs and Lili's head popped up, her flummoxed expression almost immediately giving way to that huge, sun-coming-out smile he'd grown to love more than life itself, and she startled hustling toward them faster as all the other security peeps started in on old Ironsides, bugging her to let the kids go, at least, for heaven's sake, what did she think *they* were gonna do?

So she did, and Claire and Daph streaked through the arches and down the concourse, flying to a kneeling Lili's arms. She kissed them both, over and over and over, calling them her darlings and her babies, all her in her wonderful, wonderful accent, before her eyes—watery behind her glasses—touched Tony's.

"I suppose you want to go on, too," Ironsides muttered.

"It's okay," Tony said, feeling hugely magnanimous. Grinning so hard his face hurt. "I can wait."

He didn't have to wait long. Because moments later the woman he loved was in his arms, hugging him, hugging Josie, who kept going "Goop hug, goop hug!" and then Lili said, "I was sitting there waiting for the plane to load, and I suddenly thought, Why on earth am I going back to Hungary, there's nothing for me there, I can do my work anywhere and my damn *brothers* can close up my mother's apartment, and if…" Smiling at the girls, she cupped first Claire's, then Daphne's heads. "If you're not ready, I'm perfectly okay with just hanging out together for a while—so we can get to know each other better, yes?—and see where that takes us." She looked at Tony, her eyes soft. "That goes for you, too."

His heart swelled. "You would take that risk?"

"After what I just went through to get my luggage off the plane? I'll probably never be able to fly British Airways again. Of course I haven't exactly thought any of this through, such as how I'm going to stay here without a visa—"

Tony kissed her. And grinned. "You won't be needing any of that."

"Mmm, yes, I will—"

"Not if we're married, you won't."

Her mouth dropped open. "You can't be serious," she said. Eventually.

Tony lowered his gaze to the girls. "Are we serious?"

"Uh-huh," they both said, nodding like a pair of bobble-head dolls. Except then Claire sighed and said, "Da-ad."

Tony frowned at her. By this time, a nice little crowd had gathered. "What?"

"Aren't you forgetting, like, the most important part?"

"Um, I thought askin' her to marry me—"

"Marry *us.*"

"Okay, marry *us*…I thought that *was* the important part."

After a prize-winning eyeroll, his oldest daughter yanked him down and whispered, loud enough to hear in Montpelier, "You forgot the L word, silly."

Tony cleared his throat. "Right here in front of God and everybody?"

"Yep," Claire said with a brisk nod.

"O-kay." Then he met Lili's amused eyes and thought, *Who am I kidding? Give me a bullhorn and I'll tell all of New England.* "Lili Szabo, in the past few weeks—you don't mind if I get all sappy?"

She choked back a little laugh. "Not at all."

"Just checking. Okay—in the past few weeks, you've brought somethin' back into our lives I wasn't sure we'd ever see again. Happiness, sure—who can be around you for more than five seconds and not feel happy?—but more than that, you brought back hope. And hope…that trumps logic every time. What I feel for you is solid, and sure, and…" He chuckled. "Not scary at all, now that you're standin' here." He took her hand, holding it to his chest. "I love you, Lili—"

"Me, too!" Daph yelled, letting out an "Ow!" that echoed through the entire concourse when Claire smacked her shoulder.

"Girls! Jeez!" Tony said, then looked at Lili. "You *sure* you want to sign on for this?"

She laughed, taking the baby from him. "Yes," she said softly, squeezing his hand. "Very, very sure. Can we go home now?"

Tony grinned. "Thought you'd never ask," he said. Then he yanked her close and kissed her, to a great deal of applause and cheering.

Even from Old Ironsides, bless her grumpy soul.

Epilogue

*H*ome.

Lili realized that, before she'd marched up to the British Airways counter two months ago and said she'd changed her mind—and would they mind terribly getting her bag?—that she'd never really sorted out what that word meant to her. Just as she'd never completely clicked into that whole "purpose" thing, either.

Until two *hours* ago when she'd looked into Tony Vaccaro's eyes as they stood in front of the priest and promised to love and cherish each other forever, and he'd smiled down at her, his eyes filled with equal parts gratitude and mischief, and she saw "home" in those eyes…and in his smile and his touch and the simple but profound feeling of *Yes, this is good, this is right,* whenever the girls hugged her.

That was home. And, in her case, home *was* her purpose. Not the cooking and cleaning and daily trivia that kept a household running—although there was something to be said for that sweet sense of closeness that came from sharing the mundane—but whatever she could be for the girls, for her new husband…well. Violet had hit it dead on when she'd said it's the people we're close to who have the biggest influence on our lives, our characters.

That Tony and the girls had entrusted her with their hearts…

What a gift. An incredible, completely unexpected gift.

She heard a giggle behind her. Turning, she smiled for Claire, truly lovely in her jade colored bridesmaid dress and her new rimless glasses. "What's so funny?"

"You look weird standing in the kitchen in your wedding dress."

"Hey. I waited a long time to wear one of these," Lili said, twirling. Magda had been thrilled when Lili asked her to help her shop for the gown, a fairytale confection if ever there'd been one with its off the shoulder, beaded bodice and full tulle skirt. Just as Benny had been touched when she'd asked him to walk her down the aisle. "I'm not taking it off until I absolutely have to."

Still giggling, Claire swished in and sat at the table, staring at the paint splotches, still on the far wall. Although things had eased a great deal between them over the past weeks, Lili knew it would take time for Claire to come to terms with everything that had happened regarding her mother, to fully accept Lili as a stepmother. The wedding dress might feel magic, but the woman inside it was still only human.

"You know," the child now said, chin in palm, "I think we seriously need to paint this kitchen, already."

Tony walked in, loosening his bow tie and winking at Lili. My goodness, the man looked good in a tux. Of course, he looked good out of it, too—

"Yeah?" he said, hugging his daughter from behind and propping his chin on her head. "Which color?"

Claire looked at Lili. "Which one did you say you liked?"

She turned, trying to focus on the swatches through the blur of tears. "That one," she said, pointing to the pale blue green she'd originally liked.

"Yeah," Claire said, nodding. "Me, too—"

"Claire!" their grandmother called. "We're about ready to go…oh, for heaven's sake," she said when Claire left the kitchen, "why aren't you out of your dress yet…?"

Chuckling, Tony came up to Lili to slip his arms around her waist. "I could ask you the same thing," he said in a low voice, nuzzling her neck, and she laughed, thinking, *This isn't a fairy tale, this is real…*

The girls all rushed in to give them goodbye hugs and kisses, then rushed out again. A moment later, the front door shut and the house was theirs. All theirs. Even Ed was gone, spending the next few days with Magda's and Benny's two pups. Sleepover camp, Tony called it.

"Aren't Rudy and Violet expecting us by eight?" Lili asked as—with surprising dexterity—her husband began undoing the many, many buttons on the back of her gown.

"They can wait," he whispered, kissing her. "I can't."

Joy shuddered through Lili as the gown whooshed to the floor and her husband gathered her in his arms. "I love you," he said, and she laughed.

"Me, too," she said, melting into another kiss.

Home.

She was so there.

* * * * *

RICK'S APPOINTMENT with his attorney early Wednesday morning went only moderately better than his meeting with social services the day before. The prognosis wasn't great—but at least his attorney was going to file a motion for DNA testing. Just so Rick could petition to see the child...his sister's baby. The sister he didn't know he had until it was too late.

The rest of what his attorney said had been downhill from there.

Cell phone in hand before he'd even reached his Nitro, Rick punched in the speed dial number he'd programmed the day before.

Maybe foster parent Sue Bookman hadn't received his message. Or had lost his number. Maybe she didn't want to talk to him. At this point he didn't much care what she wanted.

"Hello?" She answered before the first ring was complete. And sounded breathless.

Young and breathless.

"Ms. Bookman?"

"Yes. This is Rick Kraynick, right?"

"Yes, ma'am."

"I recognized your number on caller ID," she said, her voice uneven, as though she was still engaged in whatever physical activity had her so breathless to begin with. "I'm sorry I didn't get back to you. I've been a little...distracted."

The words came in more disjointed spurts. Was she jogging?

"No problem," he said, when, in fact, he'd spent the better part of the night before watching his phone. And fretting. "Did I get you at a bad time?"

"No worse than usual," she said, adding, "Better than some. So, how can I help?"

God, if only this could be so easy. He'd ask. She'd help. And life could go well. At least for one little person in his family.

It would be a first.

"Mr. Kraynick?"

"Yes. Sorry. I was...are you sure there isn't a better time to call?"

"I'm bouncing a baby, Mr. Kraynick. It's what I do."

"Is it Carrie?" he asked quickly, his pulse racing.

"How do you know Carrie?" She sounded defensive, which wouldn't do him any good.

"I'm her uncle," he explained, "her mother's—Cristy's—older brother, and I know you have her."

"I can neither confirm nor deny your allegations, Mr. Kraynick. Please call social services." She rattled off the number.

"Wait!" he said, unable to hide his urgency. "Please," he said more calmly. "Just hear me out."

"How did you find me?"

"A friend of Christy's."

"I'm sorry I can't help you, Mr. Kraynick," she said softly. "This conversation is over."

"I grew up in foster care," he said, as though that gave him some special privilege. Some insider's edge.

"Then you know you shouldn't be calling me at all."

"Yes… But Carrie is my niece," he said. "I need to see her. To know that she's okay."

"You'll have to go through social services to arrange that."

"I'm sure you know it's not as easy as it sounds. I'm a single man with no real ties and I've no intention of petitioning for custody. They aren't real eager to give me the time of day. I never even knew Carrie's mother. For all intents and purposes, our mother didn't raise either one of us. All I have going for me is half a set of genes. My lawyer's on it, but it could be weeks—months—before this is sorted out. Carrie could be adopted by then. Which would be fine, great for her, but then I'd have lost my chance. I don't want to take her. I won't hurt her. I just have to see her."

"I'm sorry, Mr. Kraynick, but…"

* * * * *

*Find out if Rick Kraynick will ever have a chance
to meet his niece.
Look for A DAUGHTER'S TRUST
by Tara Taylor Quinn,
available in September 2009.*

**We'll be spotlighting a different series
every month throughout 2009
to celebrate our 60th anniversary.**

**Look for Harlequin® Superromance®
in September!**

*Celebrate with
The Diamond Legacy
miniseries!*

Follow the stories of four cousins as they come to terms
with the complications of love and what it means to
be a family. Discover with them the sixty-year-old secret
that rocks not one but two families.

A DAUGHTER'S TRUST by *Tara Taylor Quinn*
September

FOR THE LOVE OF FAMILY by *Kathleen O'Brien*
October

LIKE FATHER, LIKE SON by *Karina Bliss*
November

A MOTHER'S SECRET by *Janice Kay Johnson*
December

Available wherever books are sold.

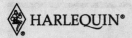

HARLEQUIN®

American ★ Romance®

The Ranger's Secret
REBECCA WINTERS

When Yosemite Park ranger Chase Jarvis rescues
an injured passenger from a downed helicopter,
he is stunned to discover it's the woman he
once loved. But Chase is no longer the man
Annie Bower knew. Will she forgive him for
the secret he's been keeping for ten long years?
And will he forgive Annie for her own secret—
the daughter Chase didn't know he had…?

Available September
wherever books are sold.

"LOVE, HOME & HAPPINESS"

www.eHarlequin.com

You're invited to join our Tell Harlequin Reader Panel!

By joining our new reader panel you will:

- Receive Harlequin® books—they are FREE and yours to keep with no obligation to purchase anything!
- Participate in fun online surveys
- Exchange opinions and ideas with women just like you
- Have a say in our new book ideas and help us publish the best in women's fiction

In addition, you will have a chance to win great prizes and receive special gifts!
See Web site for details. Some conditions apply.
Space is limited.

To join, visit us at
www.TellHarlequin.com.

REQUEST YOUR FREE BOOKS!
2 FREE NOVELS PLUS 2 FREE GIFTS!

SPECIAL EDITION®
Life, Love and Family!

YES! Please send me 2 FREE Silhouette Special Edition® novels and my 2 FREE gifts (gifts are worth about $10). After receiving them, if I don't wish to receive any more books, I can return the shipping statement marked "cancel." If I don't cancel, I will receive 6 brand-new novels every month and be billed just $4.24 per book in the U.S. or $4.99 per book in Canada. That's a savings of at least 15% off the cover price! It's quite a bargain! Shipping and handling is just 50¢ per book.* I understand that accepting the 2 free books and gifts places me under no obligation to buy anything. I can always return a shipment and cancel at any time. Even if I never buy another book from Silhouette, the two free books and gifts are mine to keep forever.

235 SDN EYN4   335 SDN EYPG

Name	(PLEASE PRINT)	
Address		Apt. #
City	State/Prov.	Zip/Postal Code

Signature (if under 18, a parent or guardian must sign)

Mail to the **Silhouette Reader Service:**
IN U.S.A.: P.O. Box 1867, Buffalo, NY 14240-1867
IN CANADA: P.O. Box 609, Fort Erie, Ontario L2A 5X3

Not valid to current subscribers of Silhouette Special Edition books.

Want to try two free books from another line?
Call 1-800-873-8635 or visit www.morefreebooks.com.

* Terms and prices subject to change without notice. Prices do not include applicable taxes. Sales tax applicable in N.Y. Canadian residents will be charged applicable provincial taxes and GST. Offer not valid in Quebec. This offer is limited to one order per household. All orders subject to approval. Credit or debit balances in a customer's account(s) may be offset by any other outstanding balance owed by or to the customer. Please allow 4 to 6 weeks for delivery. Offer available while quantities last.

Your Privacy: Silhouette is committed to protecting your privacy. Our Privacy Policy is available online at www.eHarlequin.com or upon request from the Reader Service. From time to time we make our lists of customers available to reputable third parties who may have a product or service of interest to you. If you would prefer we not share your name and address, please check here. ☐

SSE09R

Silhouette®

COMING NEXT MONTH
Available August 25, 2009

SPECIAL EDITION

#1993 TEXAS CINDERELLA—Victoria Pade
The Foleys and the McCords
When Tate McCord caught reporter Tanya Kimbrough snooping around the McCord mansion for business secrets, he had to admit—the housekeeper's daughter had become a knockout! The real scoop—this Texas Cinderella was about to steal the surgeon's heart.

#1994 A MARRIAGE-MINDED MAN—Karen Templeton
Wed in the West
Lasting relationships had never been in the cards for single mom Tess Montaya. But when her teenage sweetheart, Eli Garrett, reentered her life, it looked as if this time they were playing for keeps. Could the carpenter and the Realtor build a home…together?

#1995 THE PREGNANT BRIDE WORE WHITE—
Susan Crosby
The McCoys of Chance City
When Keri Overton came to Chance City to tell Jake McCoy he was going to be a daddy, he wasn't there. But the town gave her such a warm welcome, she stayed…until Jake returned, in time for nine-months-pregnant Keri to make an honest man of him.

#1996 A COLD CREEK HOMECOMING—RaeAnne Thayne
The Cowboys of Cold Creek
Home visiting his ailing mother, CEO Quinn Sutherland was shocked to find snooty ol' Tess Clayborne caring for her. In high school, Quinn had thought the homecoming queen was stuck up—but now he found the softer, gentler woman irresistible….

#1997 BABY BY SURPRISE—Karen Rose Smith
The Baby Experts
As a neonatologist, Francesca Talbot knew a thing or two about babies—until it came to her own difficult pregnancy. That's when she turned to the child's father, rancher Grady Fitzgerald, to provide shelter in the storm…and a love to last a lifetime.

#1998 THE HUSBAND SHE COULDN'T FORGET—
Carmen Green
Abandoned by her husband, Melanie Bishop took a job as a therapist…and immediately fell for her amnesiac patient Rolland Jones, whom a car accident had transformed inside and out. What was it about Rolland that reminded her so of the husband she'd loved?

SSECNMBPA0809